The Griffon Trilogy
Part I

ISBN 1-931391-91-2

Published 2001

Manufactured in the United States of America.

Booklocker.com, Inc.
2001

The Griffon Trilogy
Part I

Douglas & Andrea Murphy

The Griffon Trilogy

Part I

Chapter 1

On a humid August day at dusk, a beautiful woman in her twenties drove recklessly down a winding country road outside of Baltimore, Maryland in a navy, 500 series BMW. Her hands were sweating from fear, and repeatedly she glanced into the rearview mirror toward the empty road behind. Every once and awhile her car raced by a tumbledown house with a pickup truck and children playing out in the yard. For the most part the road coursed through acres of forest and open fields.

She started to relax. When she glanced into the mirror, the empty road stretched behind, and eventually she allowed the car to slow to a speed just above the limit. Suddenly her face grimaced with pain and intense fear. Once again the yellow porsche, pursuing rapidly, appeared in the rearview mirror. Her car already raced more than 15 miles per hour above the speed limit. Nevertheless she pressed the gas pedal down further, and the car jumped forward climbing to nearly twice the speed limit. The tires screeched around curves, and still the yellow porsche began to get closer.

Her body braced with alarm. Up ahead a curve too tight for her speed jarred her into action. She applied pressure to the brake and slowed down to a level she thought was safe, but something unanticipated happened. The curve was strewn with gravel, and the car began to spin out of control. Reflexively she applied the brakes even harder, but the car spun furiously around and around until it hit an embankment, and her body flew out of the side door rolling over and over until the right side of her head hit a tree and her body lay inert in the grass as a pool of blood gathered beneath the back of her head.

The noise of the accident attracted the attention of the people in the only house around. The woman inside and her children ran out to see what was going on. A small boy, barefoot, found the woman's body lying in the grass by the tree and ran to his mother who called 911 while the others gathered around wondering what they could do to help the poor woman stretched out before them.

A few hundred yards from the accident the yellow porsche at first had continued forward, but as soon as the people came out of the house it stopped dead in the road. After a minute, it turned around and sped away in a hurry.

Sara Pence, a young and vivacious nurse with her brown hair tied back in a bun, caught sight of Dr. John Bishop striding quickly down the carpeted hallway of the Rehab unit. He struck her as impossibly handsome with his athletic, 5 foot 11 inch frame, and wavy, chestnut hair often falling boyishly over blazing blue eyes that had the open innocence of a child. The man, however, seemed completely blind when it came to women and their attraction to him. Sara had had a crush on him since the rehab physician joined the hospital several years ago.

"Dr. Bishop," she yelled after him.

The doctor turned and stopped, trying to discern who had called him.

"Over here."

For a brief moment they huddled in the hallway.

"The new admission is here."

"Head injury?"

"Yes. Eva Bentley."

"I'll see her in a minute," and off he went to answer a page.

Shortly thereafter in room 6B he came to the bedside of a young woman who had just had a single vehicle car accident a few weeks ago and pulled the curtain around them.

"Hi. I'm Dr. Bishop," he said to her and a man by the bedside. "I'm one of the attending physicians on the rehab floor. I'll be taking care of you while you are here."

The woman forced a smile that, due to some weakness in her face, came out somewhat askew, but nevertheless the flawless white teeth drew immediate attention to her rather striking beauty. Long, silky black hair swept from her head down around her shoulders framing a face, heart-shaped and irresistibly attractive as stunning, hazel eyes darted around the room with quick intelligence.

" Miss Eva Bentley?"

"Yes," she said softly.

" Tony Bentley, her brother," the man beside the bed said extending his hand. John shook it briefly, and the man left the room to allow John to finish his exam. Tony Bentley was of medium height, had black hair, short and bushy, and dark eyes that stared with discomforting intensity.

"Now, Miss Bentley, I will need to get some information from you. So if you will bear with me I will go ahead and get started. We have a lot of territory to cover. I understand you are 28 years old?"

She nodded.

"Right handed?"

"Yes."

"Car accident?"

"Eleven days ago. I was in a coma for two days. I don't remember the accident at all."

"I understand you didn't injure your spinal cord?"

"Right. I fractured some bones in my neck but my spinal cord is ok. I have to wear this brace though."

"Any other injuries?"

"Yes. They say my brain was bruised, and now I can't move my left side very well."

With her right hand she pulled the covers down just enough to reveal a left arm that was pulled up against her chest. Her hand remained clenched in a tight fist, but she could push her arm out slowly and with a lot of effort. The left leg functioned somewhat better.

"Do you have feeling on the left side?"

"I do, but it's not the same as on the right. Sometimes it hurts to touch my left arm."

Dr. Bishop continued for the next hour until he had completed the history and physical examination. She appeared quite stable even though she was only two weeks from her injury. Eva Bentley came from a wealthy family in Boston. During a trip south she had wrecked her BMW as it skidded off a road around a curve. The workup in the emergency room included a brain scan which showed bruising and scattered areas of bleeding in the right side of her brain. Thus the woman had weakness in the left arm and leg. The report from the social worker showed a past history of high educational attainment and spectacular scores on intelligence tests. Undoubtedly, the accident and brain injury compromised those abilities. Later testing would show the problematic areas more precisely. The adjustment for this woman would not be easy. Understanding her injuries would take some time.

After the physical examination John chatted briefly with Miss Bentley and then excused himself and left to write notes and orders. Her deficits would slowly improve but not go away. Aside from the nervous system damage her health was impeccable.

Later in the day at 6pm John drove home feeling relaxed. His unit was filled with patients with disorders ranging from stroke to orthopedic problems to head trauma, but none of them, at least for the time being, had any acute medical problems such as infections or chest pain or acute respiratory difficulties. As a result the feeling of relaxation reached a delicious sense of comfort. His small car sped along the highway and then branched off into suburbia and finally into his own neighborhood which was older and shaded with a canopy of large oak and maple trees.

And what had the past few years been like?

After medical school and residency he had worked in a poor Appalachian town for a year before choosing to be part of a rehab practice in a moderate sized, community hospital in Maryland. A small amount of research and a role in the training of residents added extra excitement to his days. He savored his current independence and growing financial solvency.

His mother had asked, 'Why are you moving so far from home?'

'It's only three hours away from you at most.'

'But you've got everything you need here.'

'It's not the same. For work, I have a great practice opportunity including the chance to do a little research and train residents. And for pleasure, the ocean and beaches are always nearby and there are lots of waterways, harbors, boats and seafood restaurants. It's a fun place to be with a warmer climate. I want you to visit all you want or, better yet, why don't you move down here?'

That was not the answer she had wanted, and, sadly, she had turned away not wanting to let her only son go, and the prospect of living alone without him filled her with sadness.

College and four years of medical school had cost him slightly over $100,000 in debt. In the few years since residency frugal, living had allowed that amount to drop by half. With financial solvency on the horizon, the dream of a family with kids and pets and lots of neighborhood involvement began to take shape.

In the first year at this hospital he thought he had found the right woman, someone he had fallen in love with and wanted to marry. Somewhere between his inclination for stubbornness and her mercurial dynamism the relationship had veered out of control. Eventually, despite their genuine love for each other, they had splintered apart leaving bitterness and hurt feelings. His dreams and very much his heart were broken.

As he entered his house pandemonium broke out. Two dogs, Humphrey, a dalmatian, and a somewhat silly looking Italian spinone hunting dog named Groucho greeted him. They whirled, barked and pranced in their traditional "Welcome home, John!" dance that never failed to split his face in a wide grin of delight. He quickly dropped his briefcase and immediately dedicated the next twenty minutes to romping and rolling with them before finally heading back to the kitchen. On winged paws and filled with joyous anticipation, Humphrey and Groucho followed closely behind.

After presenting them with their delectable evening repast of meat by-products, compliments of Alpo, John watched them for a moment in silent reflection. He had quickly recognized the deep void in his life after his painful breakup and instinctively sought to fill it for the sake of his own self-preservation. Not wanting to get trapped in a hasty rebound situation with another woman, he had chosen instead to enroll in the local SPCA foster care program. Humphrey and Groucho were the first unclaimed charges to find a safe harbor in his home. He loved every minute. He had adored all animals since he was a boy and had even considered, albeit briefly, becoming a veterinarian. Now, he was deeply grateful for their comic companionship and the sorely needed respite from medicine.

Nearly a week passed since his return home on the day of Eva Bentley's admission. Late at night, quiet reigned in his neighborhood. In the darkness of his house as he lay sleeping, his beeper suddenly chirped madly. Muttering to himself and feeling groggy he reached over and checked the number. The nurses on the rehab floor were calling him. With great effort he got up and dialed the number.

"Dr. Bishop."

"Code blue on Miss Bentley, Dr. Bishop!"

" Did the code team come?"

"Five minutes ago."

"Be there in ten."

He slammed the phone down, dressed and ran out of the house. Within eight minutes of his page he was striding away from his car in the hospital parking lot. The yellow porsche in a visitor's spot hardly caught his attention in the quick dash to the Rehab floor and Miss Bentley's room, which now contained a stern crew of hospital personnel. An intern did CPR on her chest. The crash cart stood beside her. A medical resident stood at the head of the bed with the paddles set to shock her heart back to life. Eva Bentley's eyes pointed to the ceiling.

"Everybody back!" the resident yelled. He placed the paddles across her chest. As the electricity buzzed, Miss Bentley arched and then collapsed on the bed.

"Asystole."

Grim thoughts raced through John's mind and a single conviction arose: she's not going to make it. Right after arriving he blended into the fury of activity of the code working resolutely toward her revival, but inside himself his intuition, honed from past experience in ICU's, told him the woman could not be revived. The resident defibrillated the patient once again. The irregular pattern of ventricular fibrillation deteriorated into a flat line. In a last ditch effort to save her, the chief resident inserted a needle directly through her chest into her heart and injected epinephrine.

"What's on the EKG?"

"Flatline."

"Continue CPR."

After awhile the code leader terminated the efforts and pulled the bed sheet over her head.

Before they were covered, the lifeless eyes, staring fixed and dilated at the ceiling, sent John into a numbing sense of shock and disbelief. The room lay in disarray. The crash cart stood at the side of the bed with the EKG machine. An IV bag hung from a pole that moments before had dripped saline into the port of a central line above the woman's collar bone. Wrappers from innumerable IV meds and syringes lay all over the bed. The nurses and the doctors began the weary process of cleanup and documentation. For the residents this code might be one of several that lay ahead of them on a night of call. Along with the others, mostly dressed in green scrubs, John filed slowly out of the room.

Apart from the numb sense of failure came the long list of responsibilities that lay ahead of him and that would stretch until daylight. Notes, of course, had to be written. The most difficult duty of all required him to deliver, in the dead of night, some most unexpected and tragic news to a long list of family members. Beyond this moment in the days ahead, all of the hospital protocols would leap from their silent positions in notebooks on forgotten shelves and compel everyone into a frenzy of activity. The situation would come before the hospital morbidity and mortality review board.

Some basic questions would raise their menacing heads from the beginning and wouldn't be answered until the end.

Could the death have been prevented?

Was a mistake made or was something overlooked in her care?

The answer to both questions came with utter clarity.

No.

The answer was not an evasion of guilt or responsibility. There was simply nothing in the time she had spent on the rehab unit that would have hinted at tonight's fatal outcome.

He didn't remember any warning signs that he might have missed or ignored. She had spent her week on his floor in a relatively stable state. Nevertheless guilt and some anxiety welled within him. He couldn't help that. Autopsies fairly often revealed details that almost seemed to change the past. Just as often autopsies did not clarify anything at all and only served to intensify the mystery surrounding a death. Some families blamed the health care workers and system no matter what the circumstances, and for these people there was no peace and no appeasement. In some cases a lawsuit ensued.

People began to disperse. John conferred with one of the nurses who had been on that night.

"Can you tell me what happened?"

The nurse looked at him a moment before responding.

"Around three in the morning Miss Bentley's call light went on. Through the intercom we asked her what was wrong and she asked if someone could come in to arrange her pillows as she had come awake and felt uncomfortable. We sent in Carmella, the LPN. Carmella said that Miss Bentley was in no distress at all, was smiling and very polite and grateful that Carmella had come. Just out of the blue she had a stricken look on her face and stopped breathing. Her heart had stopped. From the very beginning there was no pulse and no respirations. First we called the code team and started CPR, and then we called you."

John stared at her, dumbfounded. Events like these occurred, rarely. One of his patients had fallen into a dreadful abyss beyond his medical skills, beyond any medical skills whatsoever. The sense of loss swallowed him up like a gray fog.

After consulting the chart he dialed the number of the brother he had met the first day. The brother was listed as the person to call in an emergency.

"Hello, Mr. Bentley?"

"Yes?"

"This is Dr. Bishop.Your sister…"

"Is she ok?"

"No, I'm afraid not. Her breathing and heart stopped tonight. Suddenly. The code team was right there in minutes. I regret very much to say she died. I'm sorry. We did everything possible."

Silence.

"If there is anything at all I can do, please let me know. Again I am truly sorry."

"My sister died?" A long pause. "Do you know why?"

"Unfortunately, not at this point. The results of the autopsy might tell us. Perhaps we'll know then."

"Yes. I have to make some phone calls. Good-bye, Dr. Bishop."

"I understand."

The brother hung up. Frustrated, John cursed under his breath. His efforts to console the brother fell short of his hopes. Not only that, the tone in the brother's voice seemed to say, 'I accuse you, doctor.'

Other relatives were called. All reacted with the same stunned silence and then the whispered confirmation half to themselves. The work continued through the night in the same manner until dawn began to break. When all the various duties had been addressed and after working late into the afternoon of the next day, he headed home with his head swimming with fatigue and stress.

Instead of sleeping he paced around his house, both exhausted and at the same time at red alert from the events of the evening. The brother worried him. From the moment John had informed him of his sister's death, the brother's voice had assumed an angry and accusatory tone. In the evening he turned on the TV and absently watched the news and drifted into a fitful sleep until he awoke early the next day still in his armchair with the TV blaring before him.

The following day the chief of staff of medicine, Dr. Lenker, approached him somberly.

"Hi, John. I'm sorry to hear the news about that patient of yours, but unfortunately we're going to have to ask you to present the case at morbidity and mortality rounds. There's going to be a full review on this one. Someone from medicine will review this, also, and present it to the medical staff meeting along with the report from nursing. Rounds are at seven this Thursday."

John nodded, numbly, absently.

The next day at the nursing station, Lauren, an RN approached him.

"Dr. Bishop, did you see them?"

"Who, Lauren?"

"The lawyers."

"The what?"

"The Bentley family sent them down today and they've been swarming around like rats asking questions, talking to people, looking over records. I think her brother sent them. What are they looking for? Nobody did anything."

"I don't know."

Tightlipped and pale John paced briskly down the hallway.

The family began to clamor for the results of the autopsy, which Dr. Flexner performed two days after the death. The report came quickly to John, and he studied every word with both hope and fear for insight into the cause of death.

He read the report carefully as it described the different organs in cold, clinical detail until finally the summary came along with its pronouncement of causation. The final words left him feeling ambivalent.

Probable cause of death: pulmonary embolus. Probably a clot had formed in a large vein in her leg, broken off, traveled back up through the heart and then into the lung blocking the blood in that area from getting oxygen. If enough blood did not get oxygen then death would follow.

John sighed. The coroner had found a medium sized clot in the left lower lobe of Eva's lung. The heart and abdominal organs were all normal. The brain had minor abnormalities no doubt incurred during the code blue and from the car accident. There was an aneurysm in the basilar artery, which runs along the brainstem (that part of the brain that extends from the spinal cord in the neck above the base of the skull). Critical respiratory and cardiac centers maintained the life of the body in this location. The aneurysm, a weak pocket of the vessel wall, had not bled.

John reviewed what had been done to prevent such a pulmonary embolus and the list included all the interventions that were possible: heparin shots, anti-embolism stockings, daily leg and calf muscle exercises. The standard protocol had been implemented, and yet it had failed. Or had it? Had Dr. Flexner rushed the autopsy and arrived at a hasty, convenient explanation?

Chapter II

A scant four days after receipt of the autopsy report, as John stood at the nurse's station discussing one of the patients with the nurses, he became aware that the risk manager, David Pullman, sat waiting in one of the chairs staring at him and waiting patiently for him to finish his business. David was a short and stocky man with closely cropped black hair and a thick neck from his days as a high school wrestler. Horned rimmed glasses perched on his nose and exaggerated the darting action of his eyes. His movements were quick and nervous, and, like Alice's white rabbit, he was always dashing around late for a meeting.

"You want me?" John asked.

"Let's go into your office."

Once they had settled into John's office with the door closed, David finally spoke.

"It's the Bentley family. They filed suit against you and the hospital. The sheriff should be making a visit to you any day now."

"On what basis?" John's mind was going numb with shock.

"Wrongful death. The family feels she shouldn't have died and that you and the hospital were negligent."

"This is awfully fast."

"It's the brother. He's pressing, hell-bent-for-leather, to get you and us. The acute care team told him she was going to do great. With her youth and good health and the nature of the injury, she was supposed to recover fairly well and be completely stable. He figures you or the hospital must have made a big mistake for this to happen. The brother has sped up this whole process faster than greased lightening."

"How much are they suing for?"

"They're going for the jackpot."

"Refresh my memory. How much is that in this state?"

"5 million dollars. Do you have full malpractice coverage?"

"Yes, but some costs might not be covered."

"Well, we'll take this a step at a time. I've looked over the case and frankly don't see anything glaring. It looks like a case of sudden, unpreventable death which of course happens in every hospital, but, of course, we don't know how the lawyers are going to twist things around."

"I wish I could explain to the family, but I'll never get that opportunity, now that they have filed suit."

"Out of the question. Absolutely out of the question now. At some point in the near future when you can fit it into your schedule we need to go over this case in a lot of detail and you can tell me your side of the story and what you think of that autopsy report. I'm sure you'll be contacting your insurance company. The hospital lawyers are already working on this."

"Any preliminary impressions from them, David?"

" Too early. All of these cases have some clear areas and some gray areas. This family has got a lot of money and a lot of connections, and that part has the lawyers here a little concerned. Enough money and gray can turn into black."

"I don't have a lot of money to turn my gray into black."

David smiled sympathetically and put his hand on John's shoulder.

"Take it easy, John. I was just being cynical. This is not a smoking gun case, at least from what I can see. Give me a call when you can get together with me. Let's say within the next two weeks."

Two days later John and the risk manager meticulously reviewed the course of events. Again and again they put the cause of death, a pulmonary embolus or a blood clot lodged in the lungs, on the table for scrutiny. Again and again this explanation fell apart. The clot was too small, too insignificant. Had the heart's pacing mechanism gone awry? Unlikely. Almost impossible. What had killed this woman?

Hours in the library spent looking up articles on sudden death and related case reports did not illuminate this issue any further. In fact, more doubt arose. John felt stumped. The pathologist seemed to have grabbed at an easy answer, one that didn't stand up to question. His course of action stood before him. The autopsy would have to be reviewed, in person, with Dr. Flexner. The hospital had asked for permission for the interment of the body to be delayed in case a second opinion on the pathological exam was needed. With dread and anxiety, he made the arrangements.

The next day in the autopsy room John and Dr. Flexner stood, gowned and masked and gloved, over the body of Eva Bentley. Dr. Flexner had a Santa Claus body crowned with a head of unruly, thick white hair in sharp contrast to his overall dress, which was precisely managed. He had a somewhat renowned habit of muttering to himself in an ongoing dialogue that typically only he participated in. Consequently John was compelled to interrupt to ask his questions and was left feeling rude and impolite. Nevertheless he persisted despite the discomfort the entire situation gave him.

His primary feeling was one of reverence toward the woman who had entrusted him with guardianship of her health and recovery from a devastating injury. Despite all his skills, honed from years of study and training, here he stood, utterly humbled. The warmth, the vibrancy of the woman was gone, and the cold and clinical surroundings of the pathology lab made John yearn for the struggles and vitality of the rehab unit. Before him lay Eva's last physical statement, the condition of her body and organs almost as they were in her last moments, the last set of clues to explain the reason for her demise.

With trepidation and determination he looked to Dr. Flexner to guide him through the findings. The body and organs lay covered in drapes before them.

"John, most of the organs I examined were completely normal. The spleen, the liver, the intestinal tract, the heart all normal." Dr. Flexner pointed to each of these organs in turn and then continued.

"The brain is on that tray over there. There is some bruising on the right parietal lobe and some atrophy but nothing that couldn't be explained by the trauma from the original accident. The only pathological findings are in the deep veins of the left leg and in the lower left lung. Let me show you."

With that Dr. Flexner pulled away some drapes covering the left leg, which had been cut down to a large femoral vein. A medium sized clot stood out within the lumen of the vessel. Next the left lung was uncovered on a tray. This organ also had been cut into, and there a clot had lodged within a small artery. Just beyond the clot the lung tissue clearly had lost viability in a small, wedge-shaped portion.

"That seems a little small to have killed her," John said.

"You never know how one of those will affect someone. A sudden shift in blood pH, a heart rhythm gone awry. It can all happen in the blink of an eye."

Suddenly Dr. Flexner's beeper went off, and the older man excused himself and left to answer his page.

John took the opportunity to examine the brain. This organ was in a shiny metal tray with a surgical towel draped over it. John carefully pulled the drapes away. Sadness for a moment caused him to hesitate, but then something odd caught his eye. The brainstem had a strange anomaly along the main vein. Instead of the aneurysm on the basilar artery as mentioned in the report, he saw a peculiar bulge in the basilar vein just adjacent to the medulla in the lower brainstem.

Overcome by curiosity and praying that Flexner's page took a few minutes, John grabbed one of the scalpels and slit open the vessel. There in the vessel sat a small device, part plastic, and part metal. He pulled it out. A sharp, short hypodermic needle jutted out from its side, and he could tell clearly that the needle had pierced the brainstem where the respiratory centers lay, those areas that made sure that breathing occurred. Furthermore from the appearance of the mechanism the needle must have slid out of the device at the crucial moment to pierce the sensitive tissues of the brainstem.

He turned the device over and over in his hands, and then slit open the plastic covering. Inside laid a small microchip, a tiny reservoir for some kind of fluid, and then the needle, which extended from the reservoir. He managed to squeeze a few drops of the liquid from the needle into a vial and to pry away the microchip, which he wrapped in some paper and placed in his pocket. Footsteps were making their way back toward him. So he carefully placed the remainder of the device where he had found it. When Dr. Flexner returned, John thanked him and then excused himself and left allowing Dr. Flexner to continue his work and his muttering.

Chapter III

John's silver sedan darted with great speed and ease through the midday traffic. The tiny microchip weighed heavily in his pocket, and the image of the device bulging through the vein with its deadly needle lying murderously within the delicate and sensitive tissues of Eva's brainstem obsessed him. Obviously someone must have placed it there. Who? Its purpose was straightforward, and clearly its purpose had succeeded. But why would such a device be used for her? The instrument was highly sophisticated. Had Eva known it was there? If so she would have lived constantly on edge, forever fearing the whims of those who had placed it within her. Now his job was to provide this piece of evidence to the police and the appropriate authorities in the hospital. Once her death had fallen into the dark realms of murder, his role quite naturally would drop into the background.

After parking he raced up to his office and put the microchip in the top drawer of his desk but put the vial with a small drop of clear fluid in his pocket to take to the lab. After shutting and locking the drawer, he dialed David's extension.

"David!"

"Oh, hi, John. You sound excited."

"I just came back from Flexner's office."

"And…"

"She was murdered, David."

"Hold on, hold on. What are you talking about?"

"Just what I said. She was murdered. I've got the smoking gun."

"Get a hold of yourself. Get a hold of yourself right now. How could Eva Bentley be murdered on a rehab floor? You're not saying we've got a psycho nurse on the unit. Because if we do, we'd better call the city police pronto and the hospital CEO and perhaps the state AG. If you're right, John, and I pray to God you aren't, these could be very bad times for the hospital."

"Stop, David. Stop. And listen. I am off the hook. The hospital is off the hook. We all are totally in the clear. Got it? Completely, let me repeat, completely exonerated."

"I'm listening, but I'm not smiling yet. I want to hear more."

"You mean see more. I've got the smoking gun in my office."

"Now you've totally lost it. What the hell are you talking about? What do you have?"

"Just get your butt down here and I'll show you."

"I'm busy all day today. I'll see you in your office tomorrow at 8 am."

"Right."

David hung up.

Tommy scratched his half-grown beard and rubbed his blood shot eyes. The warm and humid early September night relaxed him along with the bottle of gin that hung in a brown paper bag between his legs. The bottle was half empty. This spot, on the stoop of an old building, was one of his favorite places to hang out. He hated the shelter but then so did most of the homeless folks, except of course the greenhornes who didn't know any better. The street was quiet, and not a single car rumbled down the street. Probably none would at this time of night. Just as he thought this, to his surprise, a dark sedan raced to the side of a building, across the street on a diagonal from him. Two men in dark clothes burst out of the car, rushed over to the building, knocked in a window leading to a lower floor and threw something inside. Then with even greater haste they jumped back into the car and raced away. To Tommy's utter amazement the bottom floor of the building erupted with a boom into billows of orange and red flame and black smoke as shattered glass sprayed into the street. A fire raged in the bottom floor. Minutes later sirens pierced the night air.

"Fuckin' gangsters," Tommy muttered to himself with disgust. "Bastards are going to ruin this city." With a sigh, he got up took a long draw on his bottle and shuffled slowly back to the shelter.

The next day at 8 am sharp the knock on John's door sounded forcefully.

"Come in," he commanded.

David strode briskly into the room and sat down breathing heavily. As usual, he clearly had rushed over.

"OK, John what have you got?"

"It's right here in my top drawer, David. I put it in yesterday and locked it up."

"It? What are you talking about? A real gun?"

"Nope. It's a terminal device of some sort. A little tiny thing that was stuck inside the basilar vein."

"Speak English. I've been in hospitals a long time but I'm still a layman. Just what is a basilar vein and why should I care?"

"The basilar vein runs along the brainstem. The brainstem is where all the nerve connections flow from the body to the brain and vice versa but also that's where some vital centers are that control respiration, your heartbeat. Major life support systems. The main ones."

"There's no need to patronize me."

"Sorry. Well, this device had a hypodermic needle jutting out of it into what I presume was the respiratory center. A paralytic chemical must have flowed out of the device into the brainstem and stopped her breathing and her heart simultaneously, killing her. Maybe the device was triggered by a radio beacon. I have no idea. It can be analyzed later."

"Well, John, I'm like the people from Missouri. Show me, and I'll believe you. The whole thing sounds too much like some crazy spy movie. How did Flexner react? I was surprised he let you take it out of the lab."

"Flexner doesn't know. His whole story was sounding awfully weak to me. I thought, 'Maybe this guy has lost his touch.' You know? Too old. A little clot kills a healthy and strong young woman. What a stretch. So, while he was answering a page I examined the brain. I found the device and took out the tiny microchip from inside and a little fluid from the reservoir. Then I put the device back where it belonged. Flexner never caught on."

"Big mistake, John. Big mistake. You may have just destroyed a piece of evidence."

"I don't think so. If the chemical in this device matches one found in her brain, we're home free."

"Well, we'll see. Show me the microchip."

"Ok, it's right here in the drawer."

John took the key out of his pocket and unlocked the drawer but couldn't see the device. Rummaging through the papers did not help.

"What's the matter?"

"I can't seem to find it. It has to be here because I locked it up, and no one has a key but me."

A look of disgust crossed David's face. John took the drawer and dumped the entire contents onto his desk surface. The device was gone. David buried his head in his hands.

"I don't understand. It isn't here."

" I know you're under a lot of stress but promoting some cock and bull story… Really! It's a waste of everybody's time or worse. C'mon, John. Pull yourself together. This is not a Bond outing. You've got to stick to the facts. Outlandish stories like this one can only land you in a lot of trouble and end up hurting your credibility and the hospital's."

"Look, David," John snapped. "It was the truth. I didn't make anything up and I'm rather offended you don't believe me."

"Sorry, John. With a story like that you've got to deliver some hard evidence. I've got administration and the board sitting on my shoulders and frankly they expect me to stick to a very common sense approach. I don't want to hear another word about murder and secret devices. Not another word. You just might put yourself at odds with the hospital and there would be no choice as far as the hospital is concerned about whom they'll protect. I like you, John. You know that. But that is pretty much where I stand. My advice to you is to get together with your lawyers and hash this thing out. You can build a nice strategy around the facts. You didn't do anything wrong."

"What I did doesn't seem to count. The only thing that seems to count is that Eva Bentley died on my service. Her death, whatever the cause, makes me a criminal."

"That reminds me, John. The brother's got a screw loose. From what I hear he's out to make this lawsuit the vindication of his sister's death. You and the hospital, boy have we got a fight on our hands."

"So, basically, this lawsuit isn't about to go away easily, and the brother probably won't want to settle and get everything over quickly. I suppose there's no way I could talk to him and the family and tell them my suspicions to soften their feelings toward me a little?"

"Correct on all accounts. Get ready for the long haul, maybe five to eight years of slugging it out. The brother is more than just determined. Fanatical might be more accurate. Lock your doors at night. No kidding. Things have happened before."

"You mean you think he would kill me!"

"Of course I don't expect that, but you know this hospital and myself have seen a lot of strange things happen. The health profession can sometimes bring out the extremes in people. I'll give you an example. Remember the orthopedist who was shot in the chest by a patient who was unhappy with his prosthesis?"

"Yeah, I heard about that. Ok, I'll lock my doors at night. My dogs are too friendly to be of much help. I can't believe I have to protect myself from this guy. I actually feel kind of sorry for him. Somehow, in his grief the poor fellow has got the facts twisted. Kind of like a bull that's seeing red. Only I'm the damn red flag."

"Time for me to go. Remember. Both feet on the floor. Ok?"

David eyed John carefully. The young doctor had a reputation for unpredictability, and David wanted to be sure that John didn't go off on any tangents.

John caught him staring and said, "Look. I'm a doctor. Data and facts are very important to me."

"Good. Just remember that."

"Bye, David."

"Wait a minute, John. Two bits of advice for you. First, take a vacation. One or two weeks at least. Forget this whole mess. A nice vacation will tell you the world is still a nice place to live in. Then, when you come back, you'll be ready to tackle this problem and tackle it well."

David gave him a knowing glance.

"Second piece of advice. I've already said this, but I want to emphasize it. Keep away from Eva Bentley's brother, Tony. He's madder than a hornet and crazier, too. Don't talk, write or communicate in any way except through a lawyer. He'll tangle you up in legal complications faster than a spider spins a web around a fly. Well, I've got another meeting. There are meetings all day, which is just the kind of day, I hate which, of course, is every day. Bye, John. Take that vacation."

"Maybe I will. And thanks for helping me to relax," John said with a wry grin.

John wasn't sure if David caught the sarcasm. The man was halfway out of the door no doubt thinking of his next meeting and forgetting John altogether. In spite of feeling some irritation at the risk manager, John looked at him with some sympathy. The role of risk manager would bring tears of frustration to the most patient of men.

Well, we'll see, John thought. We'll just see who is out on a limb. Even though the microchip was gone John still had a few drops of fluid from the reservoir. He sent it downstairs to the lab for analysis.

The report came back two days later.

Impression:phenol.

Phenol was an alcohol highly destructive to nerve tissue. Furthermore the brainstem would show some residual of its action there. Excited, John picked up the phone and dialed the pathology lab.

"Hello, Dr. Flexner?"

"Yes?"

"Hi. John Bishop. Could I ask you to do me a favor?"

"I'd be happy to oblige in any way I can."

"Could you do sections on Eva Bentley's medulla and tell me what you find on microscopy and toxicology?"

"Can't do that," came the abrupt response.

"But you just said you would like to help me. Please it's very important."

"Impossible."

"Why?"

"There was an explosion in the lab last night and then a fire. The fire department took several hours to bring it under control. We're not sure exactly how it happened, but there's a certain janitor who likes to sneak a cigarette in the building rather than go outside. We think one of his cigarettes might have caused some of the highly flammable liquids and organic compounds to catch on fire. Eva Bentley's corpse and all the work I have done are destroyed. In fact, there's not one slide left of that woman. Not one. Of course many other bodies burned up with the fire, too, not just Ms. Bentley. Anyway, I'm temporarily in one of the old labs now. I kind of like it. Brings back fond memories."

Devastated, John barely managed to respond.

"Thanks, Dr. Flexner. Thanks very much for the information. I am really very sorry about what happened, but I have to go. Good-bye."

John hung up. Damn! Frustration and anger overcame him. All immediate hope of turning the investigations into Eva Bentley's death toward murder had vanished with the disappearance of the microchip and now the loss of her body. The timing was not lost on him. The two events followed very quickly after his discovery of the terminal device. He had to make new plans and fast. Someone had tracked his activities.

The next day, after getting a friend to cover his patients, he announced a leave from the hospital for an indefinite time. Running into him in the hall, David slapped him on the shoulder, smiled broadly and congratulated him on his good sense. 'If you only knew,' John thought. Every minute of the time off from the hospital would be used to find information to support his idea that Eva was murdered, and when he had that information he was first going to lay it in front of David. John smiled cryptically back at David as the risk manager waved good-bye.

Chapter IV

On the way home John puzzled over how to proceed. The lawyers from his insurance company would want him to keep a low profile: don't talk about the case to anyone; don't share any theories or information unnecessarily with anyone in the hospital. So, how could he find out more about Eva Bentley without anyone in her family or the hospital knowing that he was investigating her past? No clear answers existed, and the course ahead of him appeared blocked.

John turned around in traffic and headed toward the west end of town away from his home. Soon the glorious structure of the old, but restored Hotel Peronne greeted him with its promise of elegance and exquisite service and, most importantly, escape. After parking in the deck he walked quickly through the lobby up the escalator to the dark and comforting surroundings of the hotel bar with its intimate padded booths and small dark wooden tables. The hotel and bar had an excellent wine collection, but today a glass of wine did not suit his mood. The bar was empty. He went up to the bartender and ordered a martini, which he then took into one of the booths. The drink stung and jarred his senses, and soon the alcohol had worked its dangerous magic relaxing that knot of concern and anxiety in his mind. He began to unwind. The dark cloud looming over his life seemed to dissipate in these comfortable surroundings.

"Bartender, another martini, please."

The bartender nodded and soon the drink came neatly before him with its olive lolling at the bottom of his glass. 'Oh, I should have taken time off long before this,' he thought. His beeper remained silent. No patients, no family members, no administrators, no nurses bothered him. The realization brought a wave of warmth and pleasure through his body, and he took a long draught of his drink.

A woman entered the bar. Attractive and charismatic the woman sent a lightning bolt of pain and recognition through his body.

Gabby.

Dark, flowing brunette hair, long legs and emerald eyes Gabby always drew a lot of stares from men. In the meetings at the hospital where she was present John used to snicker to himself at the secret, lascivious glances of the older men of the administration. She never seemed to notice or least pretended not to notice, but more than likely she used that power to her own advantage as she was now one of the five vice presidents under the CEO of the hospital. There were no other senior, female administrators.

Gabby spotted him, frowned and then looked away. Too late, John thought and sure enough the woman strode the short distance to his booth.

"Well, if it isn't the famous Dr. Bishop. Or should I say infamous? Drowning your sorrows?" She was teasing but the edge in her voice raised his guard.

"Hi, Gabby. What's a nice girl like you doing hanging around in bars?"

"Waiting for my date. He's a little late."

"About to be stood up?"

"Well, we're as charming as always."

A headache was beginning to throb in John's temples.

"Just kidding. Care to sit down?"

Gabby stared at him for a moment. "I don't think we should break with tradition at this point."

"Sit down. I think you can safely do that. We're obviously not strangers."

Hardly. The only woman he had dated seriously at the hospital had meant more to him than any other of the few serious relationships that had passed before. Many in the hospital who watched them felt that the nice, although somewhat scruffy doctor who grew up in a middle-class, single parent household from New Jersey would never make the relationship work with the tough, smart, beautiful and exotic woman who came from an upper class family from New York.

Gabby had an unusual background. Her father, Dimitri Stavros, had arrived in New York City as an immigrant from Athens, Greece, determined to make his fortune. With immense energy and determination he worked tirelessly and eventually wound up on Wall Street and started his own brokerage firm. His hard work, intuition and intelligence helped make him a multimillionaire (a billionaire according to some), and eventually he married an aristocratic woman from Spain who was every bit as outgoing but far more fiery in temperament.

She bore him three daughters, the youngest of whom was Gabby, the apple of his eye. Nearly everyone she knew used this name, but her true name was Cristina Gabriella Elizabeth Stavros. Only her mother ever called her Cristina. The father was warm and outgoing, quite physically affectionate with all he loved, and, despite his great love for all his daughters, he especially loved Gabby. She patterned herself on him, to some extent, and wanted to be every bit the self-made success he was.

John's background could not have been more different. His mother, widowed at an early age, raised him and two daughters on a middle-class income in a well-to-do community in New Jersey. His father had been a young diplomat to Lebanon, and, in the constant turmoil there, had been abducted and killed. The son had inherited the father's restless need for travel and adventure, but the mother, recognizing this trait early on and fearing a fate for her beloved son similar to that of her husband, had curbed this characteristic as best she could.

After her husband had died she had worked for the most part to supplement the life insurance money, and as a result of her frequent absences due to work, all three children had become self-sufficient from an early age. Nonetheless all of them had maintained a buoyant sense of play, fun and achievement. John's sense of curiosity about the world burned so intensely that, at times, it had landed him into mires of difficulties. In a way his curiosity, tempered by a deep sensitivity and sense of compassion, had driven him into medicine.

"Okay. I guess you won't bite." Gabby laughed mischievously as she sat down and then leaned forward to look searchingly at John. To do so she exposed part of her ample bosom and made John feel even more awkward.

"There are some nasty little rumors running around in administration. I would like to think people were imagining things but then I am not so sure. Especially when I see you sitting here by yourself drinking martinis."

"What kind of rumors?"

"Like lawsuit rumors."

"That stuff is supposed to be confidential."

"Well, we all know how confidentiality works in a hospital."

"OK. You're right. What are people saying?"

"You first."

Gabby's sudden aura of warmth was disarming.

"Sure. But these really are secrets at this point. I can't afford to have you tell a soul."

"I've been there and back, John. I know how to keep a secret."

"Well, the rumors are right. I am getting sued and of course so is the hospital over Eva Bentley's death."

"Did you do the right things?"

"I'd like to think so."

"Then there's nothing to worry about."

"Since when were you so confident about justice in malpractice suits? Remember Dr. Olsen? An old lady he did a total hip on died. The family sued for big bucks and won. Dr. Olsen lost his practice. Everyone I knew felt he was blameless. The hip got infected with a multi-resistant bug. It was just bad luck. A product of modern times."

"Is that why you are so worried in this case?"

"No." John became silent thinking about all the events of the past few weeks.

"I'm still on your side, John. I'm not out to judge you harshly. I really think you would feel better if you told me."

The sincerity in her voice reassured him. Somewhere deep inside of her despite the animosity that lingered from their breakup lurked a loyalty and concern that was unshakable. Besides, years of hospital politics had honed a capacity for discretion that had already served her ambitions quite well.

"Okay. You win. You're lucky I'm on my second martini."

"If you have any more martinis I won't have to persuade you."

John proceeded to tell her everything including the events in Dr. Flexner's lab and particularly those surrounding the device at the bottom of Eva Bentley's brain. This latter part particularly impressed Gabby.

"Unbelievable. Of all the people to get tangled up in a situation like that. I'm not sure you're going to be able to handle this all on your own. My feeling is you are in over your head. But where to get help, I couldn't tell you. That part about David blowing you off, though, is pretty funny. That's just like our righteous, risk manager."

"He's ok."

"So with all the sharks circling around you what are you going to do?"

"I've got to get more information."

"All by yourself?"

"That's right. One of my patients was murdered. The murderer is going to get off and leave me holding the bag. My problem is that the murderer in this case isn't your usual type who uses a gun or poison or something normal. No. This murderer has got to be high tech, in fact to an unprecedented level as far as I know. In fact he is so ahead of the rest of his kind that I am going to need an awful lot of information to convince anybody that he actually exists. I am pretty much out on a limb here by myself."

"If you are right, and I am willing to grant you that you are, what you say is essentially correct. But you've got something you haven't counted on. Something formidable, I might add. " She smiled.

"What's that?"

"Me."

John looked puzzled.

"What are you saying?"

"I'm saying I want to help you, John, and you know I can."

"OK, I'll tell you what you know already. You're smart, tough, resourceful and have a great intuition, but I couldn't let you get dragged down by this. I wouldn't want you to have your life ruined because of me. I don't even know how dangerous this person or persons who killed my patient are. I am not letting you. End of story. Thanks. It was an awfully generous offer."

Gabby merely smiled.

"Too late now. My mind is made up. No more of your male chauvinism. You know, men can handle danger but women can't. You need me and I am completely fascinated and challenged by the idea. How many times in life do you get to right a wrong, solve a murder for God's sake?"

John looked at her for a moment and between his need for support and Gabby's stubborn determination he relented a little.

"You can help me as long as you stay out of anything dangerous and anything that might hurt your own life and career."

"No risks, no money. That's what my dad said. Taking risks is where it's at. Face it. We're partners. The first thing we need is a meeting to discuss what our options are. Tomorrow at 6:30 am sharp I want to see you in my favorite breakfast restaurant, O'Tooles, at the corner of fifth and Walnut."

"I'm a little surprised. That's kind of a dive."

"I like some dives. Besides this one has nearly gourmet level breakfast food. So it's not as divey as it looks. And no one you or I know in the administration would ever go there. So we don't have to worry about privacy."

A man in an expensive, dark suit walked into the bar looking around.

"There's my date. Be there, ok? I want to make a two things clear, though."

"What's that?"

"One: take a cab home. Martinis never agreed with you, and you're sounding a bit snockered. Two: our past stays in the past."

Gabby got up and walked over to the man. He leaned over and kissed her, and her face lit up with pleasure. Arm in arm they walked out of the bar lost in their attraction and infatuation for each other.

John drained his martini and ordered another. Thinking about Gabby and the other man and feeling irritated he drank that one quickly. After one more for the road he headed unsteadily away from his booth. His mind spun dizzily with the alcohol and the events of the evening. Gabby had somehow allowed a small opening in the immense fortress she had built around her feelings toward him and now wanted to help him. Up until now an unspoken rule existed between them where both would keep their exchanges to a minimum and would reserve them only for professional purposes. Gabby had managed her behavior with cold surgical precision and calculation. Although he tried to pretend he didn't care anymore, her behavior managed to hurt his feelings, and for this reason he limited his contacts with her as much as possible.

Why had he drunk so many martinis? He couldn't remember having drunk so much since college. His last serious encounter with alcohol occurred on his twenty-first birthday when his friends had taken him out to celebrate his acceptance into med school. Twenty-one drinks for your twenty-one years, they said, and surprising them and himself he agreed. Long before he reached double digits in drinks the alcohol had thrown him into raucous gaiety. Loudly he laughed and joked with his friends who roared over his antics.

Someone handed him a lit cigar, and stupidly he put the lit end in his mouth never knowing the difference while his friends bellowed ever more loudly while he looked at them wondering how he had missed the joke.

By the time he got to his room gaiety had turned to nausea, and he spent the rest of the night throwing up out of his second story window while his equally indisposed roommate held onto the belt-loop of his pants to prevent him from tumbling out of the window and into the alley below. Fortunately for both of them he kept his balance for had he lurched forward certainly he would have slipped out of his pants and fallen. The following two days required sunglasses to hide the burst capillaries in his eyes. He vowed never to drink to excess again and had succeeded until now.

Steady, he thought. Go home, sleep this off and meet with Gabby. Together, over omelettes, they could lay out his options. The cab came and met him at the elegant lobby of the Hotel Peronne and whisked him away to his home where he collapsed into his bed and fell deeply asleep while his two furry roommates snuggled closely against him.

Chapter V

The next morning found John showering in bitingly cold water, trying to shock his body and mind out of a hangover. Not too much time later he was striding into the greasy, dingy quarters of the diner known as O'Tooles searching the booths for Gabby. She yelled, smiling, from a back booth and waved him over obviously enjoying the clandestine nature of their meeting. He sat down across from her.

"I took the liberty of ordering some huevos rancheros and black coffee for you. We, I mean I, have to get to the hospital in thirty minutes. You'll love these eggs. I'm getting the seafood omelette, an absolute favorite."

"Ok, thanks. You can still order for me."

"Yup. Hey, you look only mildly hung over. It must be the Irish blood in you."

"Before the cold shower I wasn't quite as pretty."

She giggled.

The platters of food were slapped down in front of them, and Gabby began to talk and eat in earnest.

"Ok, since we don't have much time let's get right down to business. I've already figured out our first moves."

"Tell me."

"As you are probably already thinking, we've got to know more about Eva Bentley. We figure out who she was and what she was doing and most likely we have a lot of the answers to her murder. I'll take that job since I have privileged access to a lot of computer records at the hospital. Anything you do in that area is probably going to be watched pretty carefully. The next step is yours. Find out what the police report said on the explosion in Flexner's lab. Talk to Flexner. See if you can drag anything out of the old coot."

"Old coot? The man's reputation across the country is untouchable."

"He's crazy as a hoot owl from what I hear. God only knows what he's up to. I'm wondering how he missed that device, for Pete's sake."

"I was wondering about that myself."

"In any case those are my ideas. Anything you want to add?"

"Yeah."

She looked at him patiently.

"Different eggs next time. These are way too spicy."

John's coffee cup and glass of water lay empty on the counter as testimony, and tears were rolling down his eyes.

"Ok. Next time try the seafood omelette. It's out of this world."

Gabby got up and left. John left the diner and immediately headed for the police station in the jurisdiction of Flexner's lab. At the police station the officer at the desk looked at him coldly.

"Sir, I was wondering if I could get information on the recent explosion at the coroner's building down on State Street."

The police officer paused a moment.

"Dr. Flexner was the doc, wasn't he?"

John nodded.

"Ask him to see his copy of the report. He got it for the insurance. You didn't hear that from me, though," he said turning back to his work.

"Thanks," John mumbled.

An hour later Dr. Flexner was handing John the report for the insurance company on the explosion.

"I shouldn't really be showing you this, but I feel badly about the Eva Bentley case. I heard about the lawsuit," Dr. Flexner said.

John's eyebrows rose.

"How did you hear about it?"

"On the radio."

"Did they mention my name specifically?"

"Sure."

"Great. Public humiliation."

"I know how you feel. I got sued one time myself."

"How did it turn out?"

"It took six years and a lot of lawyers' fees, and we settled out of court. I didn't have the time to really fight it."

"Sorry."

"I got over it. And so will you. It's just part of the business."

John scanned through the report carefully. Traces of a plastic explosive material were found near Eva Bentley's body and some of the tissue samples.

"What about this mention of toluene. You know. A component of TNT? Doesn't that suggest arson or that someone deliberately blew up your lab?"

"I asked about that but the police explosive expert said that, with all the organic compounds lying around the lab, one would expect to find traces of that kind of chemical. The police didn't seem concerned."

"I am not sure I buy into that theory."

"I was a little skeptical at first, but once I thought about it, it made sense. Besides there is no motive. I have never heard of any pathology lab being deliberately blown up."

"How many accidental explosions have you heard of in pathology labs across the country?"

"I don't really care, John, and neither does the hospital which just wants to get the insurance money as soon as possible. The sooner the money comes, the sooner I get my research and other projects up and running. We'll get a new lab with more up to date equipment and better security, and that makes everybody happy."

John stared sadly at Dr. Flexner. He clearly had no interest in the possibility of criminality in the explosion. The pathologist just wanted to put the event behind him. The police didn't seem to care either. His beeper started to vibrate against his hip. Gabby's office number appeared on the small screen, and John bid farewell to Dr. Flexner and dialed the number from a pay phone in the lobby.

"Hey Gabby, what'd you find?"

"Interesting stuff. How's your headache?"

"That was days ago. I am fired up and ready to go."

"Good. You're going to need a clear head. Eva Bentley has a very unusual past. She was quite a bright little penny with a penchant for secrets."

"Secrets? Go on."

" Blank spots. Empty corners. My woman's intuition is sounding alarms all over the place. We need to talk."

"The scent of danger? Maybe you should stay clear."

"Save the chivalry. When and where do you want to get down to business here?"

"How about over dinner tonight?"

"You are forgetting rule number two."

"Right. Let the past be the past. I understand that, and I wasn't trying to make this into a real date. I just thought dinner would be convenient."

"I understand. Dinner, however, is taken."

"I guess we're back to O'Tooles. Tomorrow at seven?"

"Well, I see O'Tooles is growing on you." Gabby laughed. "See you at seven."

Gabby hung up.

John felt oppressively tense. Instead of going home he called an old tennis buddy, Dennis McConnel, and spent the rest of the afternoon slamming a bright, yellow tennis ball around the court. Once John had discovered tennis, the game had nearly obsessed him. That night, physically exhausted, he slept dreamlessly and soundly until morning.

At 7 am he found himself sitting once again across from Gabby smelling the dark richness of his coffee and savoring the fresh scallops and shrimp in his omelette.

"This is a vast improvement over the huevos rancheros," he said. "Now tell me. Just what is so interesting about Eva Bentley's past?"

"Just about everything. Eva's parents, Jeb and Sara Bentley, were Boston bluebloods. Jeb was an ambassador to Hungary and Eva spent the first 6 years of her life in Hungary before coming back to the United States so her Dad could take a job as a political science professor at Boston University. At the age of 6 she was fluent in both English and the very difficult Hungarian language. Unlike most young children this fluency never left her. Eva then followed a stellar academic course and graduated from high school, second in her class, held back only by a slight weakness in math and science. In the liberal arts she was untouchable. In high school, Russian became her third language."

"Family connections and a drop dead academic record clinched an admission into Radcliffe, her Mom's alma mater in Boston. She continued her liberal arts education, adding fluency in Czech and German. Her third year was spent at a Hungarian University. She used the summer to tour Eastern European countries."

"I hear they are pretty dismal places to visit."

"It's all in the eye of the beholder, but I would have to agree. Those aren't the usual places that would beckon to an attractive young woman. "

"I have had friends present papers in some of those countries. Words like interesting pop up but so do gray, dismal and depressing."

"My sister went there. It's not as bad as you think. Anyway, getting on with my story, after graduation all that work landed her a plum job in a Hungarian branch of a German bank. That job brought her a six figure income and some nice travel perks. Not bad for straight out of college."

"She could have made 50 cents an hour like me working over a hundred hours a week in a hospital." He smiled.

Gabby stared at him indulgently for a minute and then continued. "The big question still is: who was Eva Bentley?"

"Let's let our imaginations run wild. I think she was a spy or maybe a drug runner or perhaps a courtesan for high level politicians."

"Let's be serious."

"I am serious. Real possibilities. There are just too many gray areas."

" Perhaps. But we have very little in the way of facts. There are still a lot of things we don't know. We don't know who activated the device, how they did it or why. Perhaps she became a liability with her injury. With her head injury she might have spilled a lot of secrets that some important people would care a lot about."

"Maybe the device was preset to go off after a certain number of years no matter what. That little microchip might have all sorts of capabilities."

"Interesting idea. The device could also have been a suicide tool, kind of like a cyanide capsule, that she could take to elude capture."

"What about going to the police?"

"Try again. I think you'd have as much credibility with them as you did with David."

Gabby paused a moment and then continued.

"Are you sure that device is what you say it is? It wasn't something like a treatment for an aneurysm was it?"

"There is nothing like it in modern medicine. Besides, there was no aneurysm. Phenol isn't exactly a compound that agrees with brain tissue either."

"Just had to be sure."

"No problem. You know, the more I learn; the more I feel stuck. It's like one of those Chinese finger traps. The more you struggle, the harder it is to get free."

Gabby paused for a moment thinking hard.

"Then the idea is to get unstuck."

"How?"

"You've got to break that seemingly normal veneer of Eva's life. We both know she must have been connected to something much deeper. We just don't know what. If you can gather evidence about the connection, then the device and the possibility of murder will become more plausible to people like David and maybe even the police."

"Ok, so what are you suggesting?"

"You've got two weeks off, right?"

"Right."

"Well, I couldn't tell you this right away, but I've reserved round trip tickets to Hungary for you."

"Oh, no. It's an Eastern European place. It has a bad past, and it gives me the creeps. I don't speak the language. Forget it."

"Calm down. From what I hear the Hungarians are wonderful people. Just relax and give it a chance. Budapest is a modern city. You'll enjoy it. I got you a room at the Budapest Hilton not too far from the Danube. It costs a little extra, but I thought the luxury would make this less painful for you."

"Wow, do you move fast! However, my coffers are running low. Isn't there something I could do around here?"

"There's not much choice for you, John. The answers to Eva Bentley lie in Hungary. In addition to the bank some of your investigating will be at the University of Budapest."

"Why the university?"

"She had a close relationship with the University of Budapest where she spent her junior year in college. Also, at the university there is a professor, Ferenc Hopp, in the social science department with whom she had regular contacts. You need to talk to him and find out why. Try not to go to the bank."

"Why not go to the bank?"

"Well, I think you are less likely to arouse suspicions with Professor Hopp. Don't worry about language. He speaks English. I'll give you a list of other contacts, but Hopp is the main guy. Better go home, find your passport and start packing. You leave the day after tomorrow."

"The cost is still a concern."

"Hey, you're a rich doctor, right?" Gabby teased. "I know. An old myth. Don't worry, I can get the money for you if you want."

"No thanks. I'll manage," John said, stung.

"While you're away I'll work on Jack to ask his banking connections just what the hell Eva Bentley was doing in that German bank."

"I wish I had some of your powers of persuasion. My feeling is that getting people to open up about this woman is going to be very difficult. I'll do it, though. I guarantee you I'll do it."

"Great. I can hardly wait to hear what you have to say when you get back."

On his way home, just before getting to his house, John had to pull to the side of the road. Before him spread a chaotic array of police cars, yellow tape, television crews and curious onlookers. A short distance away one of his neighbors, Ed Turnball, stared with immense interest at the scene below. John walked over to him.

"Hey, Ed. What's going on?"

"You won't believe this, John. There was a murder last night. Look over there. Under that white cloth. That's where the body is."

"My God! Who was it?"

"I don't think you knew him. He lives a street or two away from you. Took his dog out for a walk, and somebody jumped him. A jogger found him this morning and called the police."

"The dog, too?"

"Yeah, the dog, too. Incredible. It wasn't for money, by the way. The guy's wallet was still in his pocket. Either the killer is a psychopath or it was some kind of revenge thing. The murder was especially vicious. Smashed his head in like a pumpkin."

"Makes you want to get extra locks for your doors at night."

Ed stared at him for a moment.

"What are you looking at?"

"I was just noticing that this guy looked a lot like you. Same height, hair color, general appearance. I'd be careful if I were you."

"No way. It's a random event. Most people get murdered by someone they know. This is a completely isolated event."

"I suppose your right."

"Of course I'm right. Better go. I've got a trip to get ready for."

"Have a safe one."

The next morning he placed a phone call to his neighbor.

"Hi. Is this Adam?"

"Yeah," came the voice of a seven-year-old boy.

"Is your sister there?"

"Uh-huh."

Silence on the other end.

"Hello?"

"Hi, Katie. I need to ask you a favor but only if your mother says ok."

"You mean take care of the dogs? I'll do it! I'll do it!" Katie was eleven years old, had thick brown hair worn in braids and doe-like eyes in a face full of freckles and was full of energy. Her love of dogs and animals exceeded anyone he knew. John and Katie had become fast friends.

"Thanks. But let me check that out with your mother. I'm going on a trip tomorrow but may need your help for a long time. Maybe even a month or two."

"You know me, Dr. Bishop. I'd take them forever. My mom won't let me have my own dog but she'll let me do this. She says I can foster care dogs any time I want."

"You're my pal, Katie. Groucho and Humphrey are going to be thrilled. After I talk to your Mom and she gives the ok, you can come over or I can bring them over any time you want."

"Awesome! My mom will be home in an hour."

"When I get back, I'll take you and a friend to any movie you want."

"Thanks."

"Katie. Just one thing. Don't walk the dogs at night."

"Don't worry. My mom wouldn't let me anyway."

Chapter VI

Two days later John was seated on a Malev Hungarian Airline flight to Ferihegy Airport in Budapest. After an overnight layover in Zurich, he took an early morning flight of several hours and landed in Budapest on a gray and drizzly day. A taxi took him directly to the Budapest Hilton. There in the lobby an overweight and balding man in a gray suit seemed to study him as he passed through the lobby. John quickly dismissed his own sense of paranoia even though the man's glare sent a cold chill through him. After checking in, he proceeded to his room and there gazed in awe at the view of the Danube that it commanded. The river, silvery and blue, snaked its way through the city seemingly painted to match the gray buildings and streets. Gabby certainly thought of everything and was probably taking a vicarious pleasure in his trip to an Eastern country. She had a taste for travel and an inclination toward elegance. Although she would be the first to deny the latter, this tendency turned up in nearly everything she did. Danger thrilled her to the marrow, but she was not one to don jeans and t-shirt and go camping in the woods.

'No time to waste,' he thought. 'I'll get the job done and then get the hell out of this country. Hungary already made him feel uncomfortable. He unpacked and then dragged out the list of names Gabby had given him. At the first position was Professor Ferenc Hopp in the social science department at the University of Budapest.

He dialed the number. A female voice on the other end spoke rapidly in Hungarian. John had no idea what she was saying. Blindly he blurted out Hopp's name. Silence and then a male voice.

"Jo napot. Are you Professor Hopp."

There was a long pause. Then in fairly good English the man responded.

"Yes. Who is this?"

"Dr. John Bishop."

"I do not know any Dr. Bishop."

"Yes, I know. I have come from the United States to talk to you about Eva Bentley."

"Eva Bentley?" The voice became quite bright and lively. "How is Eva?"

" Bad news, I'm sorry to say. She died recently after a bad car wreck."

"Oh, my God."

John could tell that the professor was sincerely saddened at the news.

"She was a beautiful and very bright young woman. I will miss her very dearly. Tell me, why have you traveled all the way to Hungary? Surely it is not to give me such sad news. I am wondering how you got my name." His tone, beneath the politeness, had yielded to puzzlement.

"Well, I would like to have a chat with you if possible, and I will explain all this. Could I come to your office?"

"Ah, my office is small and cramped and dismal. You are a visitor to our city. I could show you some of the sights. Budapest is known for its thermal baths. Meet me at the Gellert Hotel. They can tell you at your hotel where it is. You can recognize me as an old man with a bald head wearing a red tie."

"I'm staying at the Budapest Hilton."

"Very good choice. The baths are just down the road from you. Tomorrow, at 11am, by the front desk. Viszontlatasra."

"Viszontlatasra."

The conversation encouraged John. Ferenc Hopp sounded warm and human and certainly not the kind of man associated with powerful and dangerous organizations. Perhaps he and Gabby had misjudged Eva Bentley. John went to bed that night with a greater sense of security.

The next morning the concierge assisted him in getting a cab to the baths at the Gellert Hotel. The art nouveau establishment stood at the base of the green Szabadsaghid, a bridge whose artistry impressed John. At the entrance he had no difficulty identifying Professor Hopp.

"Jo reggelt kivanok, Professor Hopp," he said feeling sheepish trying this little bit of Hungarian.

"Good morning to you, Dr. Bishop," the professor responded. "Come. I have already paid your entry fee. Let us go to the locker and then to the baths. I do not have that much time."

A short while later they were wading through the hot, thermal pools wearing the skimpy loincloths provided and which did little in the way of maintaining modesty and privacy. No one seemed to care and certainly not the professor whose aged body floated limply in the grayish water. Steam came off the surface in wisps and added a pleasant, surreal quality to the environment. The warmth and healing effect of the baths soon had John wading and paddling around with pleasure, and the layers of tension within him slowly began to melt away.

"There is an old saying that if you push a pole through the earth anywhere in Budapest you will get these waters," the professor said. " This bath itself goes back 2000 years, and the Romans had their hands in many of our baths. I come here often. Tell me now, Dr. Bishop, why have you travelled so far to find out about Eva Bentley. Surely you do not do this for all your patients, even those that die. Doctors live with life and death, and no doctor can save all his patients. God calls some of them back home."

John was feeling quite good about the grandfatherly professor and felt intuitively that he was a harmless man.

"First of all please call me John. I'd feel much more comfortable if you did that. Secondly, I'll tell you exactly what is going on.

Miss Bentley's family has it in their minds that I didn't do the right things and that therefore I am responsible for her death."

"So," the professor finished, "they are suing you for malpractice. America is well known for its malpractice suits. My doctor friends here remark on this all the time with horror. Some of them would like to work in the United States, but this one thing puts fear in them, and they never go. In Hungary such things are basically unheard of. But that still does not explain why you are here. Continue."

"No. It doesn't. Well, at the autopsy I found a device, a man-made device, in Eva's brain that had the capacity for killing her consistent with the way she actually died. I feel confident that this device and the person who activated it were responsible for her death. I have come here to find out more about her past."

"You think she was living maybe a double life?"

"Yes."

The professor no longer looked relaxed. He looked scornfully down at the water and for a moment got lost in his thoughts.

"I do not know what her double life was. I agree with you, though, and I have always found some things about Eva very strange. She was very charming and full of laughter and fun, and I accepted her like a daughter but some things seemed very strange about her. There was a hidden side, also, that was cold and distant that I didn't like. I always thought that that side of her could do anything, even kill if necessary, and I tried to pretend it didn't exist. I have more for you than that, Dr. Bishop. I have some papers that she gave into my keeping. These papers should give you some clue. I have them in my office. Come today to my office at six o'clock when I am about to go home, and I will give them to you. I no longer want them or need them. I think I know a man that Eva killed or had killed, and your message seems to confirm that feeling. Come to my office and take these papers away so I can forget about such things when I think of her. I would rather remember just the things I liked."

"Thank you very much, professor. I am sorry that this subject is bringing you such pain."

"Do not worry about that. You will be doing me a favor. Just do not be late. I have a family and grandchildren I will need to go home to."

John and the professor then finished a leisurely hour in the baths sampling different pools of varied temperatures. They parted on very friendly terms having quickly established a friendship. John stayed on to receive one of the massages. His masseur had the physique of a retired wrestler and pounded and stretched John's body across the table with great vigor but nevertheless left him feeling remarkably refreshed and relaxed.

Later that day he was once again racing through the city in a cab to the University of Budapest for his appointment with the professor. The directions given him ultimately brought him to an old, Baroque building, gray and ivied. Entering the building he strode briskly through the hallways of musty classrooms and offices and finally to room 217. No one was around. It was after hours.

John knocked forcefully on the door. No answer. He knocked again and then slowly turned the knob and cautiously opened the door.

"Professor Hopp? Dr. Bishop."

In the dimly lit office he could make out the form of the professor who had his back to John. In the center of the somewhat dreary office sat a large, old wooden desk with some bookcases and some file cabinets. In front of the desk, closer to the door, were two, dark brown easy chairs. Papers littered the floor. The professor sat at the desk, turned away from the door, but was motionless with his head tilted to the side. He must have fallen asleep waiting for me, John thought, and quietly walked over to the older man.

John stood in front of him and gazed at his face. The gray, ashen mask of death stared back at him with eyes fixed and lifeless. John gasped. The professor. Dead! Reflexively he felt for a pulse but could already see that the man had expired at least an hour ago. Horror gave way to sadness as the memories of the warmth and kindness of the old man returned. Poor professor. Must have had a heart attack. I'd better get the rescue squad here.

No you don't. He pulled his hand away from the phone before touching it. The icy fear of murder crept into his thoughts and the sickening sensation of being set up. The professor's cup of tea lay cold on the desk. If it held poison and he alone was found with the professor, surely, in a foreign country, the courts would weigh against him. Closer scrutiny of the room revealed the signs of a hasty intruder. Drawers had been pulled open and a few files and papers were thrown around the office. Most of the files appeared to be missing.

While backing out of the office he wiped the doorknob with a handkerchief. This time he took some inconspicuous stairs and hid his face from a janitor coming up the opposite way. Sweating now he passed out the back door and ran toward the entrance of the university. Slow down, he told himself. Don't draw attention to yourself. Leave the university without drawing attention. The front gate is only a short walk away.

Minutes later a cab was whisking him back to the Budapest Hilton. I can't believe they've killed the professor, he thought. Again John felt his great and instant liking for the man and bemoaned the sadness that the professor's death would bring to his family. The identity of the people behind Eva's death, the explosion in the pathology lab, and now Dr. Hopp's death began to obsess and torment him. Apparently "they" had formidable powers to track him and his actions and surely "they" had the ability to block avenues of inquiry. Fear and paranoia darkened his thoughts. Later in his hotel room he slumped into a soft and comfortable sofa and studied the list of contacts that Gabby had given him.

The plush surroundings of his Budapest Hilton suite slowly filled him with a renewed sense of confidence and security. Thank God Gabby had chosen this haven for him from the work he was trying to do. He studied the list of contacts. The first five names all worked at the University of Budapest. He could not return there and thus scratched them out. Six remained, and one individual, a German, worked at the bank where Eva had worked and knew her. This man would be called next. The phone book held his name and address. On the list Gabby had scrawled the words, "No English." The concierge in the hotel lobby could help him contact the man.

His neck ached with tension. To relax himself he ambled down to the weight room and spent an hour there lifting weights and running on the treadmill. Back in the hotel room he stripped, took a long and hot shower, toweled off afterwards, and then stared into the steamed-up mirror regarding his own face. It stared back like an unhappy stranger gazing through the fog. Eyes tired and baggy yearned for rest.

His toothbrush sat at the edge of the sink, and with disgust he noticed an insect, a silverfish, curled up on top of the bristles. Shaking the toothbrush did not loosen the grip of the creature. It was dead and rigid. Strange that such a hotel could have such creatures roaming around. Why would the silverfish die on his toothbrush? Was it his toothpaste?

'No matter,' he thought and took the toothbrush to the living room to an aquarium where two large and chubby goldfish swam around.

"Here you go, little friends," he said to them. "I hope you like this little bug."

With that he flicked the insect onto the water, and one of the goldfish swam lazily to the surface and gulped the creature down. The fish, with its bulging eyes and rounded stomach, wiggled away. Within seconds, however, it began to swim erratically. Seconds later it began to swim sideways before floating, belly up, on the surface. It took less than two minutes for the fish to die. John stared at the fish bouncing lifelessly on the surface. He poked and pushed the fish with the toothbrush in his hand, stupefied, and soon after the brush had swirled around in the water a little bit the other fish began to swim erratically before floating lifeless, belly up, on the surface.

He ran back to the bathroom and flushed the brush with water for five minutes before throwing it in the trash and washing his hands thoroughly. No surgical scrub was more thorough. His heart thumped madly.

The phone rang.

John froze.

Gingerly, he lifted the receiver.

"Hello?"

A thickly accented, gravelly, male voice spoke.

"Dr. Bishop?"

"Yes."

"You should have never come to Hungary, Dr. Bishop."

"What do you mean?"

"What do you think I mean? You are here not too long, right? A man is dead. Professor Hopp is dead."

"Are you from the university?"

"Do not ask questions. I want to talk to you. Now, you are thinking: Can I trust him? You can not trust this country any more, my friend. Meet me in 30 minutes at the Angelika Café because, quite frankly, on your own you are going to die. Leave immediately. I see you there. Look for a man with a dark mustache and ask for Rudolf."

The man hung up.

Trembling John put the receiver back. Look at the mess Gabby had gotten him into. It was 8:30 pm. ‘Ok, Rudolf,’ he thought, ‘I’ll come and see you, but, before I do, I’ll let the concierge know where I’m going and who I am meeting and then ask her to send a cab at 10 if I don’t come back. If I don’t come back she can call the police, and Rudolf can go to hell.’

Quickly he dressed and went down to the lobby before grabbing a cab to North Buda and the Angelika Café.

Chapter VII

In the dimly lit café a few patrons milled about staring at the various pastries and desserts behind glass counters. John sat at an obscure, marble-topped table toward the back. A waitress came and spoke to him in Hungarian.

"I only speak English," he said.

She stared at him blankly.

It was too late for coffee but it was the only Hungarian word he could summon.

"Kave."

She nodded, smiled faintly, left and returned shortly with a steaming cup of very strong coffee.

Thereafter, a tall man, broad shouldered and burly with short black hair, a thick mustache and intense, small brown eyes, walked toward him.

"Rudolf?" John whispered, and the man swung onto a chair at his table abruptly.

"Dr. Bishop," the man muttered in the same rough voice recognizable from the phone conversation. "Did you come with anyone?"

"No."

"No one followed you?"

"No."

"No one knows where you are?"

"Not really."

"Not really?"

"Just the concierge. I had to let her know because I didn't feel safe in this meeting."

"That was stupid, doctor."

"Thanks."

"Very stupid. You can not trust the concierge."

"I don't trust you."

"That is a shame. There is much at stake here besides your life and my life. You will have to forgive me if I am brusque with you. I need to jar your senses awake. You have stepped on the tail of the dragon and you do not know it."

"I was beginning to get that impression on my own. Who are you anyway?"

"I can not tell you that. Besides it is not in your interest to know. Nor mine. I give you three messages. Because of your blunder this will have to be very quick."

"Tell me. I have travelled thousands of miles for information."

"One. I am from an underground organization at the University, a very small group of intellectuals. We are fighting what we believe to be some very dangerous technological developments or perhaps you could say the dangerous applications of these developments."

"By your government?"

"Not really."

"Not really? What the hell does that mean?"

"That's all you need to know. Point number two. Dr. Hopp had two degrees, doctorates in sociology and biology. He did all his research in biology and became famous for it. That's why Eva Bentley found him useful."

"How did you know about her?"

"She is very important. A key player as you say."

"Tell me more about Eva. That's who I really want to know about."

"Point number three. The forces in this country, against which I fight, know about your trip and your purpose. For them you know too much and thus now they want to kill you. Assassination is one of their strengths. Stay more than two or three days here and you are a dead man. So my last message is, get out. Fast. Take the next plane out of here. Now I must leave the Angelika and so must you but separately from me."

"You came just to warn me?"

"Yes."

"But why do you care about me?"

Rudolf stared at him coldly.

"I would like to care about you, Dr. Bishop, but I don't have that luxury. No. Your lawsuit situation in America is important to us. If you die then the lawsuit and your investigation dies and that would not be good for us. I am here to get you out of Hungary alive and to give you important clues to help your investigation along."

"And what clues are they?"

Rudolf sighed wearily.

" Once again. Ferenc Hopp was a world class biologist doing research with very powerful applications and potential, and that is why Eva Bentley made him her friend."

"She used him."

Rudolf shrugged his shoulders as if to say what else? From beneath the table he pulled a brown, letter-sized envelope and pushed it over to John.

"What's that?"

" Take it. It will help your investigation. Now I am going. Leave five minutes after me. Goodbye."

The large man got up and walked briskly out of the shop without looking back.

John stared after the man disbelievingly and then stuffed the envelope, as best he could, into the front pocket of his pants. The waitress came and brought him his check on which he laid 200 forint.

"Why should I believe this man?" he thought. Rudolf jumped into his life with threats, insinuations and without the least desire to establish his credibility. On the other hand the man's words impressed him with their sincerity and passion. John thought about the situation a long time. The concierge would be sending the cab at 10pm, and it was now 9:20 pm. The café was pleasant and quiet. The clientele was interesting to watch, and, for the moment, being out of the hotel in a strange city was an exciting prospect. The greatest danger had been back in his room. He motioned the waitress over and then stood up and led her to one of the glass counters and pointed to a delicious-looking chocolate cake creation, a piece of which the waitress soon laid before him. She added the price to his bill, and John put 600 more forint down, eating slowly, hardly tasting the cake and thinking hard.

Explanations for Rudolph's words and actions flowed through his mind. Quite simply, the man could be delusional, mentally unbalanced and had managed to latch onto John to foster his delusional system. Or, to the contrary, Rudolf was a cold and hardened criminal, somehow connected to the silverfish episode and was sent either to finish off the job himself or set John up for someone else in the streets.

10 pm. The café was closing, and the employees there looked at him now and then to see if he was leaving. A cab should be coming for him sent by the concierge according to his instructions. Casually he left the café nodding thanks to his waitress. He stood out on the sidewalk waiting. Five minutes passed and then ten. After twenty minutes all hope for the cab had vanished. No matter. He would walk back to the hotel. Hell, it was only a short distance away, and a walk through this ancient, intriguing city with buildings and landmarks that were centuries old would be invigorating. The Danube lay to the east, and his hotel stood to the south and west – not too far. The walk would feel good.

Crossing the Frankel Leo Ut at a light, he noticed a car coming towards him quickly. The light was red, but the car raced through it toward him, picking up tremendous speed with its engine whining from the strain. It was a heavy, dark sedan. The car was seconds away from obliterating his body. The driver's face appeared to him, and John stared at him with horror before adrenaline surged through his body. With one instinctive leap he jumped clear landing painfully on his shoulder on the sidewalk and then rolled away. The car jammed over the curb missing him by inches and then slammed awkwardly into the street in a burst of sparks from the under carriage which scraped against the asphalt.

John sprinted away. His shoulder ached and throbbed but he ran hard anyway. The car had screeched to a stop and was now turning around to come after him again. It turned the corner to the side street he was on just as he ducked behind some bushes. The sedan cruised slowly with men peering out of the driver's side and the passenger's side. The light of a streetlamp caught the blue glint of metal in each of the men's hands. John barely discerned the shapes of gun barrels.

The car passed. John sprinted in the opposite direction. His plan was to return to his hotel room, pack his bags, and leave immediately for the airport. He looked at his pocket map, noted his current position and the position of his hotel and plotted his return route. Good. The hotel was less than a mile away. He quickly pursued his course back.

Just as the Matyas Templon or Matthias Church came into view, the sound of roaring engines reverberated through the street. Behind him, in the distance, the dark sedan stood motionless at a light.

He ran for the old, Gothic, 13th century church and ducked through the front doors and down the main aisle and sat several feet into a pew and bowed his head.

Ten minutes passed and nothing happened. Relief. On the floor embedded in stone was a plaque covered with Hungarian writing, the names of two kings and the years 1867 and 1916. The kings had been crowned in this church on those dates. His eyes glanced around the altar, and then, in a somewhat uncharacteristic moment, John prayed. He prayed for safe passage back to the United States and then for the spirits of Eva Bentley and Ferenc Hopp. Two human beings. Assassinated.

The silence of the church broke as the front doors creaked into life as they swung open and then shut. Footsteps sounded on the stone floors first in the foyer and then as they made their way down the main aisle. The footsteps, slow and heavy, stopped even with his pew. John buried his head in his arms as if deep in prayer. Silence. He turned his head and looked. The round and smiling face of a short peasant woman looked back at him. She turned and sat in the opposite pew.

Relieved, John quickly got up and dashed out of the church. There was no pretense of normalcy now as he ran for all his life to the Budapest Hilton. There it stood with its fantastic Baroque architecture. He stood there surveying the hotel and the surroundings carefully. Nothing but quiet lay all around.

An explosion rocked the air. The percussion thudded against John's ears and body with a menacing violence. At about the level and location of his hotel suite, orange, yellow and black flame burst from the side of the Budapest Hilton as glass and debris rained down on the ground below. After a pause, people poured out of the lobby entrance yelling and screaming. Alarms rang. In the distance sirens pierced the quiet that previously had shrouded the city.

A car came racing past him and then disappeared toward the north. It was the dark sedan. The men inside took no notice of him but, instead, peered singlemindedly forward.

Rudolf's warning to get out of the city rang in his head. John could only think of getting to the airport and catching the first flight out of Hungary. He didn't care which country it was going to just so long as it was leaving this Godforsaken place. His passport laid buttoned into his left back pant pocket, and Rudolf's envelope poked a rumpled end out of his front pocket. He felt for his wallet, which bulged from the right side. Police cars, ambulances and firetrucks began to converge on the Budapest Hilton in a garish array of flashing lights and sirens. John turned and left. The Alba Hotel wasn't too far, and he made his way there where the man at the front desk helped him to call a cab, which came in minutes. The driver drove like a madman talking excitedly in Hungarian during the whole trip. By his gestures and intonations John guessed he was talking about the explosion, and John felt very thankful that he couldn't understand a word of what the man was saying. John knew that, as soon as the police identified the location and occupant of the blown up room, they would be looking for him in a very urgent fashion. The trip to the airport normally took forty minutes at a fast pace but somehow the driver made the trip in thirty minutes. The cabbie looked to him for which airline to stop at, and, through gestures and simple Hungarian words, John managed to get him to stop at the main terminal.

After paying with a generous tip, John walked hurriedly into the main atrium, which was relatively vacant at that hour. He walked around and scanned the list of departures for several different airlines and discovered a host of destinations none of which appealed to him. Finally, there was one that left for Rome at 4 am, and a ticket was purchased for that flight. In Rome he was sure he could get a flight to New York or, even better, to Baltimore. The moment came to pass through customs. There was no line.

To the customs officer he said, "I only speak English."

"Passport please."

John turned it over to the man who had some sort of printed communication before him. The official finished reading the report before turning his attention back to John.

"Have you anything to declare."

"No."

"Why did you come to Hungary?"

"I came as a tourist."

"Where did you stay?"

John hesitated.

"Where did you stay?" the man repeated.

"The Hotel Alba."

"Have you no bags?"

John hesitated again.

"No. I mean yes. I sent them ahead of me to Rome."

The man eyed him skeptically.

"You sent your bags ahead of you? That is unusual."

"Well, you see, not for me. I like to travel light. I don't travel well in planes. You know, airsickness. And I have a fear of flying. I don't want to have to think about too many things."

The man was frowning.

"Where are you staying in Rome? Where did you send your bags?"

"Oh, nowhere special. Just to my hotel."

"Which hotel."

"Umm, the Hilton."

"The Hilton?"

"Yes."

"I didn't know Rome had a Hilton."

"Oh, yes, a very nice one."

"You like Hiltons?"

"Well, I'm staying at one."

The man was silent for a long time. Finally he stamped John's passport.

"Can I go?"

Bored the man nodded imperceptibly. The thought occurred to John that Rome might not actually have a Hilton. Sheepish and grateful to be free he passed through to the gates.

It was 12:30 in the morning. His plane left at 4am. Until then John needed a place to hide. There was an all night bar close to his gate and he took a seat in there. Two men, obviously drunk, talked loudly a few tables away. John ordered coffee and didn't dare try to sleep until safely on board the plane.

Back in Maryland Katie eyed Groucho and Humphrey with pleasure but also a little bit of concern and guilt. Her friend, Megan, had come over today and in the excitement of having someone over, she had forgotten to take the dogs out. However, night had fallen and it was dark outside. Both Dr. Bishop and her mother had told her over and over not to take the dogs outside at night, but now, if she didn't, they might go to the bathroom in the house. Her brother was watching TV while her mom and dad were in the kitchen talking. Just this time. Just this one time. Quietly she leashed the two dogs that bounded in anticipation. Outside the street was quiet. Slowly she led her two companions along the sidewalk up the block until they had taken care of their business. Headlights approached from down the road, and soon a nearly windowless, dull white van had come up even with Katie. A man poked his head out of the window.

"Nice dogs," he said. "What're their names?"

Katie eyed him scornfully and began to walk toward her house. The van kept even with her.

"What's a matter? Cat got your tongue?"

"Nope. I don't talk to strangers. This one's Groucho and the other is Humphrey."

"Good names. Look. We're ok. Do you know Dr. John Bishop?"

Katie hesitated a minute.

"Maybe."

"Seen him around recently?"

"No. Why're you askin'?"

"Just curious. Say, could you help us?"

"What kind of help?"

"We're lost. Could you tell us where the nearest gas station is?"

"Just go down that road and take a left."

"You know, that's great but I tell you, I am really bad with directions. Why don't you come in here with your dogs and show us. We'll take you right back to your house."

Katie picked up her pace. Tears were forming in her eyes.

"No."

"Is that any way to help a stranger? It'll just take a minute."

Katie started to run. The dogs galloped ahead with pleasure while the van stopped, and a man came out and ran after her. She turned into her yard to the front door, but the man ran ahead and blocked the door to her house.

"I want you to turn around and come with me," he said. Katie looked at him with fear and remained motionless. The spinone started to growl and bark at the man, and soon the dalmatian barked and growled as well.

"Get rid of the dogs, and you won't get hurt."

The man started to approach her, but the dogs now barked furiously. The front light came on and the man ran. The front door opened.

"Katie, get in here. What did I tell you about walking those dogs at night? Don't ever let me catch you doing that again."

"Sorry, Mom. A man was bothering me."

The mother's face registered shock and then alarm.

"Where darling?"

"See that van?"

Her mother ran into the street as the van roared away.

"We'll see what the police have to say about this!" her mother muttered furiously as she marched toward her daughter.

Together they walked inside.

Chapter VIII

A rat scampered out of the cell of stone and metal bars. The dungeon was dark except for shafts of light that pierced through the dank air heavy with mold and dust. Footsteps fell noisily down the hallway. Soldiers and a priest were coming for him. The time had come for his execution. His bones and muscles ached from the cold. His dark brown wool covering scratched at his skin. He was hungry and thirsty. No matter. Sometime before nightfall he would be dead. The soldiers and priest stopped in front of his cell. Awkwardly in his armor one of the soldiers unlocked the door of thick iron rods and then nodded to the priest who, without hesitation, entered the cell. The priest was a large man, bald and heavyset. His eyes were light blue and shone with fierce intensity and even, the prisoner thought, a trace of compassion. He sensed the priest thought his verdict unjust but the priest would never voice such discontent and would never deviate from his assigned task. With perfect attention to ceremony the priest delivered last rites to him and left. Then the soldier entered, unchained him from the wall and pulled him outside where two others bound his wrists tightly behind his back.

Roughly they pushed him forward, and the entire group, except for the priest who had left now, marched forward out of the dungeon and into the courtyard of the castle. There he was loaded onto a wooden cart with others to be taken to a public square where the executions would proceed. The King, by his own request, would be present to witness the completion of their sentences. Because of the King many soldiers now waited on horses in long lines of two in front of and behind the carts of condemned men. Horns blared and the procession began to move forward.

The day was gray and dismal. Large dark clouds gathered in the sky, and light rain fell now and then. Thunder rumbled in the distance. If he had to die certainly this day should be his last when the world appeared hostile and threatening. The man next to him smelled of sweat and urine and filth. No one spoke. It was forbidden. A soldier would come and thrust a spear or sword through the chest of any man that spoke. Some men looked around absently with eyes filled with despair whereas others had eyes filled with almost uncontrollable fear and searched their surroundings restlessly for an avenue of escape or for a soldier who might show compassion. But the soldiers stared impassively ahead. Each condemned man by virtue of his sentence had become a non-entity, without rights and without value. He wondered how the others had arrived at this point. His own life had followed a relentless course to this moment although that insight was only apparent to him in rctrospect.

John awoke on the plane with a start. Somewhere over the Atlantic, in the dead of night, the jet flew smoothly along at 30,000 feet. The cabin was quiet except for the occasional snores of sleeping passengers or the hum of equipment. In two hours his plane would land at Kennedy airport, and he wondered if the trouble in Hungary had followed him to the United States. For the next two hours, the cabin would provide a protected haven from both his difficulties in Hungary and those in Maryland. Relaxed as a cat before a blazing hearth he fell asleep.

Two days later, back in his house and feeling more rested and certainly safer, John called Gabby at her office.

"Hi. I'm back."

"John. I didn't expect you back this soon. How did it go?"

"Lucky to be alive. Somebody nearly blew me out of the universe."

"Are you serious? That's terrible! Did you get hurt?"

"No."

"Thank God. Don't expect me to cheer you up with news from the hospital."

"What do you mean?"

"Sorry, I can't talk now. Got a board meeting in five minutes. Meet me tomorrow morning at O'Tooles. I haven't been there since the last time we went. My boyfriend doesn't like that kind of place."

"Right. See you then."

"Bye."

John felt a knot in his stomach. Something obviously was going very wrong with this lawsuit, and now he had to wait until tomorrow to find out. Should he call David? Forget it. David would sermonize and admonish but would not give out information. Worry mounted within him, and to divert his thoughts he called a nurse, Michelle, whom he had casually dated in the past, to come join him for a football game later on in the evening. Michelle had become more of a friend and pal in and out of the hospital and usually enjoyed impromptu outings. She was a short, quick woman full of energy.

That night, the stadium was packed with students, and the excitement was infectious. The smell of hot dogs and popcorn, the roars from the crowd and the fierceness of the competition on the field as well as the warmth and friendliness of his friend buoyed John into a sense of optimism. After the game they climbed into his car and started to drive away from the stadium and traffic.

"Ok, Michelle, what next? Want to grab a drink somewhere?"

"Sure, let's go to that restaurant that overlooks the water."

"Schooner's?"

"Yeah. I think a friend of mine might be there. Jennifer."

"How's she doing?"

"Not bad. Except she wants to get out of the CCU. The stress is getting to her. All of the new documentation you have to do and the short lengths of stay are starting to bother her. She thinks the patients are leaving before they really ought to."

As Michelle continued to talk John could feel his spirits sink. The hospital gossip suddenly brought the weight of his situation down upon him and left him despondent.

"What's the matter, John? You're not saying anything."

"I know. I'm sorry. I think I am going to have to go home. I've got a lot of things going on that I can't talk about. Sorry."

Michelle stared at him in mild astonishment. Something really must be wrong for John to behave this way. She had heard some of the rumors about the lawsuit and now, in a maternal gesture of support, extended her arm and put her hand on his shoulder.

"Not a problem, John. Some other time."

Guiltily, he dropped her off at her apartment. At home he tried to sleep but tossed and turned until morning, when, feeling tired and stale, he once again found himself sitting across from Gabby at O'Tooles.

"So what happened over there?" Gabby said. She was picking up a piece of syrup- soaked pancake with her fork.

"You go first. I couldn't sleep last night thinking about your bad news."

A vague look of sympathy appeared.

"This is pretty bad, John. I don't like it one bit. Apparently Eva's brother is trying to instigate a criminal suit against you as well as a malpractice suit."

John's appetite disappeared. His fork fell from his hand. The knot in his stomach had returned.

"You mean like manslaughter or something? Like something I could go to jail for?"

"Yeah."

"Is that possible?"

"In this state, yes, it is. The chances of such a suit succeeding are slim, but nevertheless the whole situation is risky."

"Goddamnit! Well, what can I do about it?"

"You'll have to get a lawyer outside of your insurance company, one with more experience in criminal litigation."

"What will the hospital do about this? Will they take away my privileges?"

"The board is not sure what it will do. The whole situation is being discussed. They're getting an outside panel of doctors to review the whole case. If these doctors find any major fault you could be out."

"Can this get worse?"

"I won't answer that. So far David has been your supporter, believe it or not. He thinks you're getting a raw deal and are basically innocent."

"He hasn't changed his mind about my story has he?"

"Hardly. That story made him feel sorry for you. He saw you as some sort of pathetic soul grasping at straws, who could use a helping hand, and David is kind of like that."

"You're not feeling that way are you?"

She eyed him wryly.

"Nobody as smart as you would make up such a story. David is too dumb to realize that. In one way this doesn't matter. The brother can do whatever he wants. Your job remains the same. Dig up information on Eva and get the murder idea to stick. You've got to give that whole idea a plausible background."

"Before we go any further, I've got to tell you what happened in Hungary."

"Go ahead. Tell me you got some really good information and found the city incredibly romantic."

"I got a little bit of information from a strange guy named Rudolf, and no, the city wasn't romantic. It was goddamned dangerous. I would have liked it better if I weren't running for my life most of the time."

John then proceeded to tell Gabby about the events in Budapest including the grill session from the customs officer who had nearly, he thought, blocked his exit from the country.

"I think if you had waited even one day they would have never let you out and you would have been sitting in some federal, Hungarian jail waiting for your trial."

"Waiting and rotting. Yeah, I think you're right. Rudolf gave me this paper by Ferenc Hopp. I don't know what it's about. It's in Hungarian."

John passed a brown envelope over to Gabby.

"I'll get it translated."

"By your boyfriend, the financier?"

"You're very quick. He's a merchant banker. His business is international. Getting a translator is no problem for him."

"While your boyfriend is getting that done, I think I'll catch up on things at the hospital. My career is going to hit a freefall if I don't."

"Don't do that."

"I don't give a damn what anyone thinks. I've got a right to do my job."

"Well, the hospital lawyers, whom I've been grilling on your behalf, tell me you could end up in jail if this criminal indictment goes through. Frankly, John, you don't have the time. If you end up in jail you won't have the opportunity to dig around in this business of Eva Bentley. If you don't dig up some good information, the criminal case and the malpractice case are going to be a lot harder to defend. If you lose those two cases, a lot of other things can fall down on you."

" Are you trying to make me depressed? Because if you are, you're doing a very good job."

"Don't take it personally. I don't want to hide anything from you. You're going to have to take some risks. As you can see, people are upping the ante all the time. But that goes for me, too. If the hospital figures out what I'm doing, my career is finished. They will, too, eventually, but I'm betting that by that time it won't matter."

"Listen, Gabby, I want you to get out of this while you can."

"It's already too late for that for reasons I don't have time to explain. You've got to press forward, John, and succeed."

"Ok, ok. I'll press forward."

"Good. And now for your next move."

"Another foreign country?"

"Not this time. No, I think you'd better go up to Eva's alma mater, Radcliffe, which merged with Harvard a few years back, and poke around there a little bit. Talk to some of her old professors. There is one, a Professor Stanhope, who had some connection with Ferenc Hopp. Hopp was a visiting professor once at Eva's alma mater up around Boston, and apparently Stanhope helped get him there."

"Is Stanhope a biologist?"

"Nope. Historian. Asian/Chinese studies."

"What's that got to do with Hopp?"

"Don't know. Maybe you can find out."

"I'll drive up there. I can use the university library to dig into some of Hopp's papers. I'm having a hard time imagining what Eva the banker wanted from an elderly, academic biologist. What did he have that she needed? "

"Put that on your list, too."

Gabby paused and then added something cryptic.

"You've got a lot of friends in New York, don't you?"

"Yeah, so what?"

"You might be getting a chance to see them. There's a consulting group up there that might be able to help you out. Don't ask me any more questions, though. I'll tell you more when you get back."

The breakfast drew to a quick close. Gabby rushed back to the hospital leaving John who then spent the rest of the day making arrangements for the trip north to Boston. In the late afternoon he made a quick phone call to check on the dogs and Katie.

"Hi, Katie, how're you doing?"

"Fine."

"Are the dogs ok?"

"Oh, yeah. They're doing great. I want to keep them."

"Talk it over with your mother. That's a lot of responsibility to take on. You're not walking the dogs at night are you?"

Katie hesitated.

"No. I mean I did once. But that's all."

"Anything happen?"

" Some man in a van asked me for directions, but Humphrey and Groucho started barking and scared him off."

"Look, Katie. You've got to be really careful. There are some bad people who are not very happy with me that might be roaming around the neighborhood."

"My mother read something about you in the paper. Did you do something bad, Dr. Bishop?"

John sat startled for a minute.

"Uh, no. Some people think I did but it is all a big misunderstanding. I'm trying to straighten it out now. Listen, maybe it would be safer if I took the dogs back now."

"No!" Katie said emphatically. "I'm having so much fun with them, and they protect me!"

"Well, ok. Just be careful. If it's alright with you and your mother, I'm going to have to depend on you a little bit longer."

"That's great. I can't wait to tell Megan. She wants to keep the dogs if I don't."

"Thanks, Katie. You're a real pal. Talk to you later."

"Bye, Dr. Bishop. Be careful."

By the early evening his bags were packed and his reservations were made at a hotel near the University campus beginning the following night.

After the long drive to Boston, he checked into his hotel, a nondescript building tucked into one of the quieter side streets. The next morning, a quick call brought Professor Stanhope's secretary on the line at the nearby university.

"The professor is not in his office right now," she said. "You can catch him at his next lecture. Ten this morning in the basement auditorium at McClellan Hall."

An hour and a half later, John slipped quietly into a seat toward the back of the lecture hall, which was only half full. Students sat in blue jeans and sweaters and sweatshirts scribbling notes busily in their seats. Professor Stanhope had already launched into a discourse comparing the old China and the new China, which was attempting to fit into a modern, global culture. The professor spent a lot of time explaining how new technologies were altering both military capabilities and social structures.

"So you see," he continued, "China is attempting to preserve its insular nature and control over its population and yet participate in the global economy. Some groups, the political dissidents you hear about, are trying to speed up this freedom of interaction. There are also some that you don't hear about that have taken matters completely into their own hands. They operate underground utilizing the black market to have a worldwide economy and a social structure within the official one of China. These groups have been termed criminal organizations, and the authorities of China and of governments around the world are trying to stamp them out as rapidly as possible. The groups have reacted with strict internal discipline and ruthless enforcement techniques which are effective and have made them all that more powerful."

A student in the front of the class raised his hand.

"Aren't these gangs a danger to the freedom of people in legitimate democracies?"

"Of course that would be a concern. However, I did not mean to talk about this issue today," Stanhope retorted and then digressed into a completely different subject. The question seemed to irritate him.

The class ended. The final exam was in two weeks, and John felt fortunate he could skip that part of this course. At the podium Stanhope was busily packing notes into his briefcase in an attempt to rush out to his next appointment.

"Hi," John said smiling and extending his hand. "I'm John Bishop. I'm a doctor from Maryland. I wanted to ask you a question or two."

The professor looked puzzled.

"I take it you are not here to inquire about pursuing undergraduate studies?"

"There was a former student of yours, graduated from here a few years back. She was a patient of mine, and I need to get some background information on her."

"Lots of students come and go here, doctor. I wish I could remember them all, but I don't." The professor looked disgruntled and suspicious.

"If any student should stick in your memory, she should. Her name is Eva Bentley."

The professor looked shocked but quickly tried to hide his emotion. His expression turned cold and serious.

"Doctor, I'm sorry. That name means nothing to me."

"Look. I've got a picture. I can tell you about her family and what courses she took with you. Let's see if that helps."

However, Stanhope was beginning to walk away.

"Sorry. You seem to know a lot more than I do. I really am in a rush. Have to pack for a trip. Call my secretary if you want. Goodbye."

The professor disappeared out a back door, and John stared after him both stunned and disappointed. Later that day he called the office number.

"Professor Stanhope's office."

"Yes, this is a Dr. Bishop. Is Professor Stanhope there?"

"The Professor is not in right now."

"Do you know when he will be in?"

"Professor Stanhope had to leave town suddenly. He won't be back for at least two weeks. Professor Dillon is covering. Would you like to talk to him?"

"No thanks. Could you tell me if an Eva Bentley was ever a student of Professor Stanhope?"

"I'm sorry, sir, we are not allowed to give out information on students."

"Could I call him at his hotel, wherever he might have gone?"

"Professor Stanhope is travelling to Hong Kong, sir."

Dead end. What was the connection between Eva and Stanhope? Eva had been so stunningly beautiful. On that basis alone any professor probably would have remembered her. He promised himself he would look into the publications of this professor as well at the university library.

Later that evening he sat in his hotel room with two stacks of articles on his bed. One consisted of Professor Stanhope's publications, and the other stack held those of Professor Hopp. One by one he browsed through them. Stanhope had published a lot on trade between the western countries and China. Many of his articles had been cowritten with law school professors with an expertise in international trade law or with business school professors who specialized in international trade in Asia.

Hopp, on the other hand, in his early works, had put out a lot of research on cellular genetics. He had developed a lot of technology for gene splicing. From there Hopp seemed to have branched into work involving the embryos of mice, rats, pigs and other animals. Hopp's discoveries had proceeded in genetic engineering with the speed of his brilliant mind. Innovations accumulated that left the rest of the scientific world looking on in wonder.

So what did a bench level geneticist and an Asian history professor with a fondness for the subject of trade relations with China and other Asian nations have in common? Nothing, as far as John could tell. No two men seemed further apart than Stanhope and Hopp. He had liked Hopp, but Stanhope turned him off completely.

Fatigue overtook him. There in his hotel room with the night table light on and amidst a disarray of papers, John lay down in his shorts and T-shirt and fell asleep. An odd, disturbing dream unfolded. Two men entered his hotel room. The men were large and quick, and before John could arise from the bed, one of them stabbed a needle into his shoulder and injected a yellowish liquid into his muscle. Within minutes the room grew fuzzy and distorted. His body swayed erratically, uncontrollably, and the men helped him to his feet, dressed him and took him outside. They murmured something about drunkenness to the night clerk and laughed maliciously. The night clerk stared uncomfortably at his computer.

In the parking lot they dumped him into the back seat of a SUV before climbing in the front and driving off. John's body grew heavier, and he became nauseous. The man in the passenger seat reached back and gave him a different injection painfully into his buttocks, and John fuzzily wondered if the man knew enough to stay away from his sciatic nerve. The second injection caused him to pass out. From that moment, on the events proceeded in a patchwork fashion as his consciousness drifted in and out. There he lay on a gurney being pushed down a narrow hallway that seemed to rock side to side. Next he was in a room, and a man's voice was talking to him telling him something important over and over. He drifted in and out and always the man's voice resounded in his mind authoritatively, insistently. Now he was back in his hotel room, and the two young men were dumping him into his bed laughing at jokes at John's expense. The dream seemed to end then except for scattered recurrences of the man's voice droning like the ceaseless buzz of bees inside his head.

Next morning he awoke overwhelmed with nausea. His head pounded, and his body ached as if elephants had trampled it all night. Moaning he crawled out of his bed, bent over, and rushed to the bathroom where he promptly threw up several times. Trembling he made his way back to his bed and fell into it.

"I have to get out of Boston." The thought came with unexpected urgency.

Slowly and painfully he began to pack his bags. The mere thought of Eva Bentley sent his body into spasms of pain and tension. His mind reacted with fear. Like a wounded animal relying on gut instinct, he made his way back to Maryland.

At home that night he felt much better and began to get ready to go to bed. For him the Eva Bentley affair was over. His involvement was finished. Gabby would hate him for this decision. But what could he do? He climbed into his bed to the comfort of familiar sheets and surroundings. His mind was drifting, and before the thought of Gabby could disturb him any more, his breathing became slow and regular and his body sank heavy and relaxed into his bed. Sleep overtook him. For the first time since Eva's death, peace surrounded him.

The wooden cart rocked uncomfortably over the dirt road. The procession had entered the town square and throngs of people waited expectantly for the executions to unfold. The King always held these in a public place. The current of fear they generated among the populace helped to create the appropriate level of obedience, fear and respect for the laws. Rebelliousness and resentment were also generated, but ultimately those who manifested these emotions were discovered and brought to prison. The executions took place on a simple, stone plaza as the King and his subordinates looked on. Many soldiers surrounded the entire perimeter. People outside of the procession were allowed to watch from a distance safe enough to protect the King from the arrow or rock of some would-be assassin. There on the square stood the executioner, tall and massive, covered in a black robe and hood waiting for the first victim. The first man was brought up quickly. The guards had to carry and drag him for his legs had been broken the night before in torture. Soon the square was covered in blood. A light rain began to fall and wash the blood away into the straw and dirt. A guard grabbed his shoulder and began to pull him to the executioner.

Chapter IX

"What? What did you say, John Bishop?" *Gabby asked* incredulously, angrily. "What the hell is going on? What exactly happened up there at Boston?"

"Nothing. That's the whole point. Nothing. I tried to talk to Stanhope and he didn't know what I was talking about. He thought I was crazy. What's he going to think? A doctor drives all the way up from Maryland, sits in one of his classes and then starts asking him about a former student, one he has no recollection of."

"I don't believe him. It sounds suspicious."

"You're always suspicious."

"I have to be."

"Well, frankly, I don't know. I just don't know. It was very strange. I woke up the next day after seeing Stanhope and felt nauseous and terror-stricken about the whole thing. A terrible foreboding. Sometimes instinctively you know something. My instinct is telling me to quit. Once I gave into my instincts, I could relax. I just get the feeling that something bad is going to happen to you and me if I keep this up. I could tolerate something happening to me but not to you. Not to you, Gabby."

"And this change of heart came about just like that? Nothing happened?"

John shrugged.

"Nope. Saw Stanhope. Went to the library and got some articles. Read some of them in the hotel room. Went to sleep. When I woke up I knew what I had to do."

"You're holding out on me."

"There was a strange dream. That was the only other thing."

"Oh yeah?"

"Yes but it was nothing. Stupid. Pure anxiety. Two men came into my hotel room. Gave me a shot and drugged me and then dragged me off somewhere."

"And then what happened?"

"Nothing. I don't remember. It's not important. It was just a stupid dream."

"By the way why don't we go over the translation of the information Rudolf gave you? It's pretty weird info, but I need a doctor to help me out with it."

"Naw. Why bother? Even the thought of touching any of this stuff makes my hands sweat. I'm taking that as a sign."

"John, this is so unlike you. Something must have happened. You just don't remember. You'd better get over it fast, though. Your problems are multiplying every day it seems."

"I just don't agree. You and I, we'll just have to agree to disagree. You're being overdramatic."

"Think about it, John. I'll get back to you later. Don't make a big mistake."

Gabby hung up. She had been very persuasive, and his hand hesitated for a moment on the telephone. He wanted to call his lawyer. After a moment, he pulled his hand away. For him the best strategy now would be to forget completely about the events swirling around him. Let his mind lapse into some kind of oblivion. Perfect. There was a small house on the ocean, very isolated, that a friend of his owned and rarely used. A small dirt road led to it. The house had no phone, no TV, no radio. It barely had electricity. The surf was rough, and in the bedroom at night the briny ocean air and the steady pounding of the waves on rock and sand drew one into that careless happiness of the beach. He would go there. He called his friend who confirmed that the place was empty and available. Tomorrow, after packing a few belongings he would leave for a long weekend, maybe even a whole week before coming back and starting work again.

Later that day in the early evening his bag lay packed and ready in the trunk of his car. The news on TV was running through the day's litany of tragedies, and John turned it off. In the kitchen he poured a glass of orange juice and slowly drank it. The doorbell rang. For a moment he froze. That strange terror now associated with Eva Bentley sent his heart pounding with adrenaline. A thought occurred to him, and he relaxed. Probably his friend was dropping off the key to the beach house. He walked to the front door and opened it.

Gabby stood there with a man whom at first he didn't recognize and then realized he was someone who worked at the hospital.

"Well, John, are you going to let us in?" Gabby demanded.

"What brings you here?"

"I'll tell you in a minute," Gabby said and strode in as the man followed.

"John, I'd like you to meet Dr. Ernest Collings. He's a psychiatrist at the hospital. You probably don't know him. He also has a private office in town and does some research with the university."

John shook his hand.

"Do you think I'm cracking up?"

"Not exactly."

"Drinks anyone?" John offered as his guests sat in the living room.

He was about to pour himself a vodka on the rocks.

"No thanks." She plucked the vodka bottle out of his hand. "And John I'd rather you not drink either. At least until you hear what I have to say."

"Yeah? That sounds ominous. This sounds like a lynching committee."

"No. We're here to help."

"Ok. You've got about five minutes before I start my own plan for relaxation."

"Fine. I'll get to the point. Ernie and I have been talking about what happened up at Boston. There was one story that particularly caught our attention."

"What's that? My feeling that Stanhope was lying about remembering Eva?"

"No. That's not it. It was the dream."

"Are you here to psychoanalyze my dream?"

"We don't think it's a dream."

John smiled.

"Well, maybe I won't need this drink after all. I have nothing to add about the dream. I don't remember any more than I told you. What can you possibly say about it? Did it express my fears and crystallize a new attitude toward my situation? Sure. It probably did. But so what?"

Dr. Collings interjected.

"I don't think it's a dream."

"Ernie's an expert in post traumatic stress disorder. One of the hallmarks is a dream that often recurs about a stressful event."

"You're losing me. I haven't had any stressful events like the one in my dream ever in my life."

Dr. Collings looked John firmly in his eyes.

"I am not saying, at least not exactly saying, that you are suffering from post traumatic stress disorder."

"Then what are you getting at?"

Gabby quickly interjected.

"Because of his experience with PTSD, Dr. Collings has the ability to understand what is going on with you which is, from what we can gather, pretty unusual and somewhat related to PTSD"

"I'm waiting with baited breath."

"Well," Dr. Collings continued, "I would say that the dream you remembered was either part of a real event or part real event, part dream event."

"And I repressed the real event because it was so awful my subconscious had to hide it from me. But imperfect defense mechanisms caused parts of the event to bubble into awareness," he said somewhat snidely.

"Not quite. You repressed the real event because you were told to repress it. Parts of it, like you said, have leaked through."

"You mean my mind has been reprogrammed?"

"In so many words, yes. More like classical conditioning techniques. You know. Pavlov's dogs."

Gabby elaborated.

"You were forcefully and with the use of drugs taken out of your hotel room to another location where terror techniques, both physical and psychological, were used to cause you to associate fear with Eva Bentley, a fear so great you couldn't bear to keep involved in the investigation."

"And why don't I remember that?"

"The drugs," Dr. Collings interjected. "A lot of drugs will cause memory lapses. The nausea. Remember? Those were the aftereffects of the drugs."

John sat stunned. A chord of recognition, of understanding, had been touched. He laughed, nervously, nonetheless.

"You guys are crazy. C'mon. I'm not even sure that's possible."

Dr. Collings looked at him sternly.

"It is possible. You know that all too well. How many of your patients who have had traumatic injuries from a car accident and don't want to drive again? Somebody artificially gave you a traumatic accident."

"Why didn't they just kill me?"

"We thought of that," Gabby said. "At this point we don't know. Obviously we are very relieved that they didn't, but why they didn't has us very concerned."

"What exactly are you proposing? I get the impression you have a plan to undo all this tampering."

"We do," Dr. Collings began slowly and carefully. "I could bring the memories out into the open where you could face them and deal with them and make them less frightening. Probably in one session we couldn't conquer all the fear, but enough work could be done to allow you to continue your investigation. Relaxation techniques and a small dose of an oral barbiturate would be used to facilitate things."

With infallible intuition Gabby walked over to him and put her hand on his shoulder.

"Don't worry, John," she said soothingly. "Dr. Collings is an expert. He's written a lot of papers in this area. I think I'd be safe in saying he's never had any tremendous problems in doing this kind of thing."

"That would be correct," Dr. Collings affirmed.

"But you never have had a situation quite like mine before, right?"

"No. But yours is not that different. The principles are the same."

"Sorry, guys. I am not about to hand my subconscious over to a perfect stranger."

"John, that is why I'm here. For the trust factor. You've got to do this. Someone has rewritten the script for you to steer you into a different direction. But that direction could be very bad for you. Let Dr. Collings do this. I'll be right here looking after things."

John stared hard at Gabby.

"I don't know. I just can't do this. It's all just a little too ridiculous. I've got a long trip tomorrow. You'd make me very happy if you would just leave me alone right now so I can get a good night's rest."

Dr. Collings leaned forward.

"Dr. Bishop, I anticipated this. The anxiety and fear are quite strong. Just remember that the medication will provide you with enough relaxation to continue. Although the events we uncover most likely will be quite upsetting at first, once you bring them out in the open you should feel a lot better. More like your old self."

Then, at those words, a part of his personality, the maverick, the gambler, rose with eagerness to the challenge presented to him.

"Alright. I'll try this. If nothing happens I can't say that I'll do it again. What do I do first?"

From his tweed sport coat the psychiatrist pulled out a medicine bottle and gave it to John.

"Take one of those. It's the barbiturate. Then lie down on that couch and take your shoes off and get comfortable."

"Here, John, take this." Gabby handed him a glass of water. A quick gulp and the pill was down. John stretched out on the couch and kicked off his shoes.

"I'll just go to sleep. Wake me when this is over."

"No you don't. Listen to the doctor."

" Gabby, if you would, please turn down the lights," Dr. Collings said, immediately getting to work. "Dr. Bishop, listen closely to what I have to say throughout all of this. The drug will soon be getting into your system and you are going to feel fairly sedated. Right now we are going to go through a relaxation process to assist with the effects of the drug. Start with your toes and feel them get heavy and relaxed." The process continued until John was breathing slowly and deeply and appeared in a profoundly relaxed state.

Gabby sat in an easy chair near John's head while the doctor had pulled up a chair facing him from a few feet away. The house was silent except for the deep, relaxed breathing coming from John and the low and resonant voice of the doctor.

"Now, I want you to go back to the night you spent at a hotel in Boston. You are there, now. Tell me what you see."

John's mouth moved silently a few times, and then his voice emerged strange and unfamiliar in a low monotone.

"I am on my bed looking over articles."

"These are articles by Professors Stanhope and Hopp. Am I correct?"

" Yes."

"Go forward now. What is the next most significant event?"

"Two men have come into my room."

"Describe them."

"Dark hair. Both are very tall, young and strong. One in particular is unusually strong. Thick arms and chest. Broad shoulders. They are joking and laughing."

"What happens next?"

"I ask them who they are and what they want. The larger one grabs me and pins me down. He says they'd better hurry before I wake up completely. The other one comes toward me with something in his hand."

"What is in his hand?"

"I can't tell at first, but then I see it's a syringe. 5cc. There is a yellowish fluid in it. I try to struggle but the man is too strong."

"Now what happens"

"The man sticks the needle through my shirt into my shoulder. It hurts. He injects all of the fluid into me. Pretty soon the strength goes out of me. My mind is in a daze. I'm limp and helpless."

John's voice had changed. His words slurred and his mental clarity clearly had gone.

"OK, John, there is a part of your mind that is unaffected by the drug but that sees everything that is going on. That part of your mind now takes over and will tell me what is happening."

Immediately his voice resumed its former crispness and clarity.

"Yes."

"Good. Now tell me what happens next."

"Each man takes an arm and a shoulder and half drag and half walk me out of the room. They're back to laughing and joking. I try to do what they say. I feel completely at their mercy, and they know that. Outside in the parking lot, they push me into a car, put a hood over my head, and drive away."

"Go forward to the next significant event."

"The car is stopping. I get pulled out of the car. The sound of waves and the smell of salt air come to me. One of them pulls the hood off of my head. We're in a remote area by the ocean on the edge of what I later learn is a cliff that drops one hundred feet or so to the rocks and waves below. I can see the lights from houses in the distance but none nearby. They are taunting, me throwing punches and kicks at me that gradually get harder and harder until my sides ache, and I am doubled over with pain. They seem to enjoy doing this and slowly are pushing me closer and closer to the cliff."

"A certain amount of terror is mounting within me about being pushed off the cliff, and they sense that and begin to feed on that. I am totally helpless to defend myself because of the drugs. In fact I fall on the ground several times, but then they pick me up and throw me closer to the cliff and kick me some more. Finally at the edge of the cliff I am begging them not to throw me over. The drugs have made me very dopey and emotional, and I start to cry. All my emotions are out of control. Fear, sadness, remorse. I know what they want. They tell me. Give up my investigation of Eva Bentley. 'I can't,' I say and burst into tears. One of them grabs my ankles and the other dangles me over the edge. Give up or we'll let go. 'Ok, Ok.' My emotions are so out of whack from the drugs that I can't control myself and give up. They pick me up like a broken rag doll, pat me on the back and take me into the car and put the hood back on."

"Where are we going, I say. 'The boss wants to see you,' one of them answers and the other reaches back and sticks another needle in me, and I pass out."

"What's the next thing you remember?"

"I am coming to a little bit but feel even dopier than before. The car has stopped. They pull me outside leaving the hood on my head. There is the sound of waves and the smell of salt air again. But I can tell we're in a less remote place. We're walking on gravel and then a long wooden dock. Then they force me to walk across some kind of plank or walkway that sways up and down a bit."

"Are you going into a boat?"

"I couldn't see it from the outside because of the hood. But they take me inside and pull off the hood. Then I could tell it was a yacht. A big one."

"Are there windows to see out of?"

"I am below decks."

"Who is around you?"

"The two men."

"What are they doing?"

"Waiting."

"What happens next?"

"Another man has come. He is leading me down a hallway while the two large men support me so I don't fall. I have trouble controlling my legs because of the drug. They take me into an office where there are two men. One of them appears to be the boss, and the others are very deferential toward him. He keeps in the shadows so you can't see his face very well. The other is a doctor or what passes for a doctor. This man motions toward a gurney of sorts. 'Take off his clothes and put him on that.' I am stripped completely naked and then placed on the gurney and strapped in."

"Continue."

There was a long silence. John's breathing became deep and labored and his head began to rock back and forth. Sweat beaded up on his brow. Gabby leaned forward in her chair quite concerned.

"John, you are relaxing now and can look upon what is happening as if you were a bystander. Tell me what you see."

"It's pretty awful. I don't want to think about it."

"Try to see this objectively. Once you confront it you will feel better. We are here to support you."

"This doctor is a complete bastard. He takes out a biopsy needle and without any anesthetic, with just a tiny swab of alcohol for sterility, jams the needle into one of my testicles, takes a tissue sample and then pulls it out. My mind is a sea of searing pain. The pain is so bad I am about to pass out."

"The doctor looks over to the man in the shadows for instructions. I know he is asking whether he should kill me or not. 'Use the drug,' the man says, and the doctor fills a syringe, and before he injects the med into me he leans over and warns me not to continue my investigation of Eva Bentley. There is the stab of the needle, and I am out. The next thing I know I am waking up in the hotel room, nauseous and aching. My groin feels like someone tried to kick a field goal there. You know the rest."

"Ok, John, you can gradually come out of your relaxed state," Dr. Collings instructed. "Start with your toes and then move up your legs and then on to your hands and arms and body and head. Do this slowly and then you can open your eyes. The drug will still be affecting you so you might want to get up slowly."

John followed the instructions and after five or ten minutes was sitting up in the couch blinking and looking all around.

"So how did I forget all of that?"

"They wanted you to forget, and they did that with the drugs. But the pain and the fear were still there along with the instructions to stop this investigation. Because you couldn't confront it, take away some of the fear, the whole situation had a real grip on you. I take it you don't feel quite that way now?"

"No. Not at all. I am ready to get back into things. I'm a little more nervous about it than before, but I want to get to the bottom of this. They could have killed me!"

"They will eventually if they get the chance," Gabby added. "They must have some purpose left for you. Maybe you should get out."

"Now wait a minute, Gabby, you're the one who got upset when I did that."

"I know. But I didn't realize how close you came. What happened to you puts a different light on things."

"To me it seems we go ahead full steam. That's the best chance all the way around. You can drop out if you want to and probably should. In a way, the more I know about this group the more confident I feel."

"Drop out? No way in hell. This group is going to get the feel of a kick in the pants from one angry Greek girl."

"Well, if you'll excuse me, I have to get back to the hospital." Dr. Collings got up to leave.

John rose and shook his hand.

"Thanks. You just saved me from making a big mistake."

"Don't mention it."

"John, I have to go, too. Are you going to be alright?"

"Yeah. I feel fine."

"When you get back from the beach we'll have to meet."

"Cancelled. See you at O'Toole's tomorrow. Same time, same booth. So, you're still with me?"

She smiled.

"I don't know who is more stubborn, you or me. The Greeks or the Irish. Of course I'll be there."

Dr. Colllings and Gabby left, and John watched them as they pulled out of his driveway. His investigation couldn't succeed without her. Yet how would he feel if something happened to her?

Chapter X

New York City. Great restaurants, horrible crime. Great culture, millionaire costs. Dirty subways, and bums slinging their arms around you asking for a quarter. The bustle of millions moving endlessly, here and there, night and day. Walk to any corner at any time of night and there is a restaurant open, half full of customers getting off work, going to work, taking a break. John took in the skyscrapers, the blaring of car horns, the sounds of people begging, playing music for a quarter, the sight of people in suits or young women with magenta hair, leather skirts, and ears, noses and bellybuttons pierced with glittering, metal rings and jewelry. New York City. He loved it. It was the most vibrant city he knew, never boring but full of the rapid swell of theater, art, medicine, sports, music, fashions and the hidden and not so hidden sway of fortunes being made and lost.

John had driven to Metuchen, parked his car there and then taken the commuter train to the World Trade Center. His car would be safer in New Jersey, and driving in the city didn't appeal to him. Now, if only he could get a cab, one with a driver who valued life over death and sanity over speed. A cab pulled up to the curb, and a man with a Middle Eastern accent leaned out of the window and told him to get in. John was headed to the upper west side. A couple of his friends were expecting him, especially someone from medical school who now was an ER doc, Bill Andreadis. Aside from Bill he most wanted to see Stacey Simmons.

"I'm not in a hurry."

"Sure, sure," the cabbie answered and raced off into the traffic as John clutched the door, white knuckled.

A short time later the cab pulled up to the hotel.

"Ten fifty."

John gave him twelve dollars, and the man took the money scowling and muttering about the tip. Next time, take the subway, John advised himself.

After he had checked into his room he made a phone call to confirm his appointment with Morgan, Morgan and Associates the next day. Morgan, Morgan and Associates came about through an inspiration of Gabby. The company provided several different kinds of consulting work to its corporate customers, but the type John was interested in involved their expertise at discovering and defending against corporate sabotage and spying. Their connections ranged throughout the world, and their reputation excelled in terms of success, client satisfaction and cost of service.

The money for his consultation, strangely enough, came from the hospital. Gabby had gone before the board of directors and pleaded his case for extra help with respect to the criminal overtones surrounding the death of Eva Bentley. The CEO of the hospital was there. Despite murmurings of dissent around the table, the CEO came down strongly in favor of the support and volunteered a consulting firm he knew and trusted. The other members stared at him disbelievingly but finally came around. Cost became an issue, but the CEO overrode this concern. The story and the evidence sounded fantastic to them, but they yielded out of fear that a catastrophic scandal would send the hospital into ruin. The CEO made clear, however, that the consultant only would look into the potential criminal implications and in no way would assist in the malpractice issues.

The next morning John found himself in his best suit taking another cab to the East Side to the cushy offices of Morgan, Morgan and Associates. These offices lay on the seventeenth floor. There was no button on the elevator to push. Instead John had to slide a coded card into a slot beside the number 17. The letter that came with the card announcing his appointment said that his card would only work once and would be immediately voided after the first use. John slid it through, and the elevator door closed quietly. The elevator rose quickly. A receptionist's desk lay close to where he got off.

"Hello, I'm Dr. Bishop. I have a 9 am appointment."

"Yes," said the young woman smiling sweetly. "That would be with Mr. O'Brian. Room 14. Two doors to your left. He's waiting for you." The woman paused to gaze at the handsome doctor, but he had already turned to go.

The door to room 14 gaped open. Inside a dark haired man in a gray suit, club tie, and conservative blue shirt sat hunched over his desk.

"Hi. May I come in? I'm Dr. Bishop."

The man looked up. His serious expression melted and he smiled warmly.

"Dr. Bishop. I'm Larry O'Brian. Nice to meet you. Come in and please have a seat."

John sat down in a very comfortable leather chair. After some pleasantries were exchanged Mr. O'Brian came to the point.

"As you know, Dr. Bishop, the Board of Trustees of your hospital has hired this firm on your behalf. Normally we don't take individuals as clients. However, the CEO of your hospital is a close friend, since college, of one of the partners, Julius Morgan. Mr. Morgan is taking a special interest in your case. I hope that makes you feel you have some support in what must be a very trying situation."

"That is good news. Thank you."

"Now tell me everything that has happened. Try to include as many details as you can. Our conversation will be recorded, later transcribed and then reviewed by a research team. Every lead and angle will be hunted down through the nearly unlimited resources of the firm. I can assure you that our resources are quite extensive and reach throughout the world. Take your time. Tell me as much as you can remember."

"Ok. There is a lot to tell. Let me gather my thoughts for a moment."

The two of them sat there in silence for several minutes before John finally began to speak. He started with the first day he met Eva Bentley and took her history. Mr. O'Brian sat silently, listening intently and never interrupted him to ask questions except once, when John talked about Rudolf.

"What was that comment he made?"

"I'm not sure what you mean"

"You know, something about a dragon. Tell me exactly what he said. I don't want to put words in your mouth."

"He said that I had stepped on the tail of the dragon but didn't realize it."

"He used that phrase, 'tail of the dragon?'"

"Yes."

Mr. O'Brian sat back for a moment thinking hard.

"It may have been a deliberate reference."

"You mean some kind of a clue?"

"Um. Maybe."

"Well, tell me. It really would help me to know."

" There is a group, a criminal group, that has the nickname, 'Tail of the Dragon.'

It's a group that spans the globe and is involved in many different things. According to legend, anyone outside the group only sees the tail. If you see the dragon face to face you will never live to tell the tale or so goes popular folklore. By definition also the group remains mostly undefined, something of a mystery. Its main center is in China and let me tell you, the Chinese people and authorities would love to rid themselves of this scourge. In fact sometimes the Chinese police have used some of our information."

"As I said before, the reach of this group spans the globe. People have died at its hands in South America, the United States all over the world. Some people think it is one very well organized group and some think it is a loose association of very diverse groups. No one really knows. In fact some people don't even think it exists. They think that police authorities use the name to refer to criminal groups throughout the globe in a general sort of way. You know, one term for all the international crime that goes on. The firm believes in its existence. You may have stumbled onto a segment of this group. If that is the case then indeed you are a lucky man to be alive."

"What makes the firm think it really exists?"

"Oh, a number of things. Several of their assassins have been caught in such diverse places as North Africa, Holland, Indonesia and other places."

"How did you link them?"

"Partly by circumstance. All of them carry a small tattoo on the right shoulder. It's a symbol of their rank and initiation into the organization."

"A dragon?"

"No. A Chinese symbol that represents opportunity through two elements: chaos and great danger. Our information says they have perverted this meaning to the following: through darkness and chaos great opportunity is obtained. Some of the higher level assassins have an additional tatoo, waves, which is the Chinese symbol for the hiding place for dragons."

"Is that what they said under questioning?"

"No. All of the assassins died."

"How?"

"Suicide capsules. All of them are trained that if captured they should kill themselves. Let me tell you, all of them do. A very distasteful death awaits them if they don't. Aside from its other …um… traits, the organization is quite sophisticated in torture techniques, most of which are used to keep its own members in line."

"Does anything else make you think it exists?"

O"Brian leaned forward for emphasis.

"Yes."

From a bookcase behind his desk he pulled down an album of photos.

"Take a look. There are four separate, major locations. An island in Malaysia. Another island near the mainland of Greece. A villa on the Cote D'Azur in France. And a nondescript farm in Bhutan"

"Bhutan?"

"A small, mountainous country in Asia. The perfect location for meetings of the group's hierarchy. Below the ramshackle farm buildings are sophisticated meeting rooms and communication systems. The perimeter of the property is heavily guarded."

John studied the photos of picturesque islands, ships and harbors.

"What about the other three areas?"

"Regional headquarters for a legitimate shipping business which, in its own right, brings them many millions of dollars. At the same, time they can use the ships to transport billions of dollars of illicit cargo."

"Why don't the local governments investigate and seize their property?"

"The Greek authorities did that once on a tip from us. Searched every ship, every building, and every storage depot. Took all the computers and found absolutely zero. Nothing but the records and material from a legal business. They never tried again, and our relations with the Greeks have suffered ever since. As far as the island in Malaysia... Let's just say that with a local economy benefiting greatly from the presence of this company, the incentive just isn't there."

"Given the strength of this group shouldn't I be dead by now?"

O'Brian looked at him squarely for a minute.

"Quite honestly, yes. That surprises me no small amount. I can't figure it out. In any case forewarned is forearmed. You need to be extremely careful at all times. Even for awhile after all this passes."

"If it ever does."

"It will. Now continue."

John finished his description of events up until that moment. Mr. O'Brian stared off into space in silence.

"Do you think I'm crazy?" John ventured.

O'Brian turned and looked at him almost as if he were surprised to see him there.

"Not at all. I've got to say this isn't adding up for me. Prostitution rings, pornography, drugs, money laundering. That's the usual thing. Sometimes corporate spying or theft. I'm having a hard time placing Eva Bentley and the events you've mentioned into that scenario. Doesn't fit the pattern at all. Well, it's going to be a challenge for the firm. We have a file of unsolved cases, Dr. Bishop." He lowered his voice as if imparting a secret. "Let me tell you. That file is very small. This may cost your hospital a pretty penny. But from what I hear your hospital is willing to take care of that."

" I'm a little surprised. In fact I don't understand. The administration at the hospital is not exactly in a mood to shower me with all kinds of blessings."

"Who knows? Just thank your lucky stars you've got something like this going for you. I think we've taken this about as far as we can today. For the next few weeks the rest will be up to us. We'll be contacting you. If anything else evolves on your side you need to keep us informed."

"Should I call you?"

"Absolutely. Here is my card."

"One last question before I go."

"Sure. Go ahead."

"Once this is all over, assuming that happens, will I ever be free of these people, these tail of the dragon people."

O'Brian thought hard for a moment.

"Quite honestly, and not to scare you, no one who has ever entangled themselves with them, gotten on their bad side so to speak, has ever survived. But none of these people were like you, an educated man with resources from people like us. You'll make it. You're going to be ok. But from now on, for the rest of your life, you'll have to be on guard. You are on their list and you're going to stay there. They might try to abduct you, kill you, frame you or impose any other sort of ruination on you. But if you stay on your toes, don't do anything foolish, you'll be ok. I am deliberately being a little harsh here so you remember my words and take them seriously."

"I don't think I can forget a warning like that."

A short while later John left the building. He liked O'Brian who seemed genuinely warm and sincere and who also seemed quite competent and knowledgeable. Later he would have to ask Gabby about the hospital politics that caused the CEO to support giving thousands of dollars for this kind of professional help. That kind of action on the part of a hospital had to be unprecedented.

Chapter XI

About an hour later he was back in his hotel room. The message light on his telephone was flashing. In a moment a voice mail recording played back to him.

"Hi, John. How are you?" the voice oozed and immediately his heart raced with excitement. Stacey Simmons! Their friendship started in his freshman year of college and continued on and off through the years of med school and residency. Working on Wall Street she had met a wealthy man, married, had children and then had divorced a year ago and was now raising a seven year old daughter and a ten year old son, alone. John knew her as a very sexy, independent and smart woman. Some found her overly ambitious. In college he had idolized her and formed an enduring crush, but she had always seemed out of his reach and had rebuffed the few attempts he had made at forming a romantic bond. Now, oddly enough, she was calling him. The old feelings surged within and his mind danced with pleasure.

"I found out through a mutual friend that you were coming to town," she continued. " I would love to have dinner with you. I took things into my own hands and made a reservation at Tavern On The Green at eight tonight. Just leave a message on my answering machine whether or not you can make it. Hope to see you later, John."

John dialed her number and left a message that he would meet her there. His excitement continued to mount, and although he wondered why all of a sudden she had decided to call him, ultimately he didn't care. Blessed with a luminous presence that always seemed to capture the attention of others, Stacey managed to captivate, charm and entertain. These powers also at times allowed her to manipulate others although never maliciously. After a quick shower he dressed in dark slacks, a tweed sportcoat and a gray tie.

Two and a half hours remained until dinner. Fidgeting he grabbed a newspaper but then threw it down on the floor. Abruptly his mind turned to his friend, Bill Andreadis who lived at 85th and Central Park West and who was an ER doc. Bill had spent a good part of his residency working in the Bellevue ER. A thought occurred to him, and he gave him a call. Bill had just gotten off a shift and was ready to wind down and thus agreed to meet him at Café Central, a place where a lot of aspiring actors hung out. A short time later John was sitting at the bar, waiting. The big burly man with his thick black mustache and muscular arms and thick chest showed up and grabbed a stool beside him. For a while they exchanged gossip about mutual friends. John told him he had a date with Stacey Simmons later on that night.

"Oh, yeah, I remember her. Good looking and smart. Not someone I personally trust though. A little too self-serving for me. I heard she's run into a bit of bad luck recently."

"Really?"

"I think she made a few blunders on the market and got seriously demoted. The brokerage firm she worked for lost lots of money. Millions. She lost face and friends. Kind of hard up for cash now that she is divorced and on a lesser paying job. She likes an elegant lifestyle, as you know. From what I know about her she'll end up on her feet in no time."

"I doubt if she is looking for a comfortable lifestyle from me."

"No offense, John, but I don't think so either. Frankly, I don't think she'd be good for you. You should think hard about this one. She's the kind of woman who likes men who are cutting tough deals for millions of dollars. You've got too much of the poet in you. You never bought into the power trip. Don't change by the way. That's one of the reasons I like you."

"Maybe the poet who likes to play goalie for DC United."

“Yeah, yeah, yeah. I’m not saying you aren’t tough.”

“Let’s switch gears for a moment. Here’s an odd question for you. You’ve worked the ER’s in New York for some time now. You’ve seen a lot of shady characters come and go. Have you ever seen someone with a tattoo on his shoulder, one that looks like a Chinese symbol? On someone whom you might think was a criminal?” On a napkin he sketched a picture of the symbol that O’Brian had shown him. Bill studied it closely.

“ You’re right. That is an odd question. Lot’s of guys come into the ER with tatoos. It is a city hospital after all.”

“I’ll explain in a minute.”

“Let me see. I have to throw out all the types with the usual tatoos, naked women, ships, motorcycles, hearts, etc., etc. A lot of these tatoos are on the shoulders. But Chinese. I don’t know. I’ll have to really dig for something like that. Ok. Ok. Hm. Yes. Yes. You’re lucky I’ve got a good visual memory. Ok. I’ve got it. There was an oriental guy that came in, in his twenties. Must have been a martial artist. Wiry strength. Not much English. Had a knife wound into his spleen. Should have made it. No major bleeding, no respiratory problems.”

“Why didn’t he?”

“Seems like a gang had marked him. Someone in a gang had knifed him and wanted to finish off the job. Myself and the trauma team were standing around him while he lay on the stretcher when into the ER burst these gangbangers with automatic weapons. The security guys pulled out their pistols, and bullets started flying around the place. One of the security men went down. Suddenly the gangbangers left. When we got up the Chinese fellow was dead. Six bullets. Chest and head. There was no chance for him after that of course.”

“Did you know anything about him?”

“Nothing except where he lived. Seems like he was just off the boat. His accent was awful.”

"Where did he live?"

"Where else? Chinatown. I can even give you his address. When I go back to work tomorrow I'll look him up in medical records and put the address on your voice mail. I'm not sure it's an address you'll want to visit. Hey. Now it's your turn to do some explaining."

"Well, it has to do with a patient of mine who died. A woman. Sudden death. No really good reason for it. I think she was murdered, to tell you the truth, but I want that question answered once and for all."

"Murder in a hospital? Boy, I bet your hospital would like to keep that under wraps. The evening news would have a heyday. And you're investigating this possible murder? Shouldn't the police be doing this?"

"No one has seen any evidence for murder except me."

"Why do you care so much? A bunch of criminals are working out their differences. Sounds like something you should stay away from. Do I smell a lawsuit here?"

"That's part of it."

John then launched into a brief description of the events up until the present time. Bill was shaking his head.

"Hey, take the hit on the malpractice suit. At least you'll be alive. Your career might be a little less alive, but you'll still be around. There've been some doctors around here who haven't come off so well. In fact, there was one just recently who was shot in the head by a disgruntled patient. Take the hit on the suit. I don't want to hear about something tragic."

John looked at his watch.

"Thanks for the beer. I've got to go. It's time to meet Stacey at Tavern On The Green."

John walked out of the bar and could feel Bill staring after him disapproving of both his date with Stacey and his investigation. Stacey had him wrapped around her finger, and there was nothing he could do there. As for his investigation, like Gabby said, it was too late to get out. Or rather, he didn't want to get out. He wanted to settle the score.

The dinner with Stacey proceeded like a dream. She never had looked so radiant and had never spoken so entrancingly. Before long, before dinner was even half way finished, his old infatuation had flared up to a fever and with each smile, each peel of laughter and each sweep of her blond hair Stacey appeared to him like no other woman, except perhaps Gabby. But Gabby he had pushed far into a corner of his mind.

"You know, John," she said, "my ex-husband was a cruel and selfish man. He wasn't at all like you. But because of him I think I can appreciate all sorts of things about you that I didn't before. Sometimes bad experiences make a woman wiser."

"We certainly learn things as we get older. But you always had beauty and charm."

She smiled.

"Tell me, though, what brings you to New York? Medical conference?"

He frowned.

"I'm sorry. Did I say the wrong thing?"

"No. It's just that sitting here with you… I had nearly forgotten."

She leaned forward and stared into his face with eyes that sparkled with energy and interest.

"Tell me. You'll feel better." And one of her hands reached out and covered his for a moment with a warmth that spread through him in a comforting glow.

"It's a strange story. I hope it doesn't ruin the fun we're having."

And so without thinking, the story spilled from him from the day he saw Eva Bentley to his parting words to Mr. O"Brian at the consulting firm. Far from appearing bored, Stacey paid rapt attention to his words. One bottle of wine disappeared and then another. Before long they were leaving the restaurant arm in arm strolling a short while in the park and then kissing under the trees in the night before catching a cab to his hotel room where Stacey fell into his arms and both melted into a night of passion.

John awoke the next morning in a state of confusion. The clock on the bedside table told him it was 11am. The message light on the telephone was flashing. Beside the telephone lay a small folded note on hotel stationery that smelled of perfume. This latter item he picked up and read.

Dear John,

I had a wonderful night, my sweet. How long have I known you and never considered the happy moments that we could have had together. I am sorry to have left while you were asleep but the thought of my children woke me up and I remembered how much I missed them and so I had to leave and pick them up from my parent's apartment. Give me a call when you get a chance.

Love,
Stacey

John read the letter several times glowing with the warmth that came from her words. Call her? Yes! But not before sending flowers. A giant bouquet of yellow roses. Ah, Stacey. The woman was magic. Every spare moment in New York would be with her, and then she would have to come to Maryland.

The message light flashed annoyingly on his phone. Picking up the receiver he checked voice mail.

"Hey, John. Bill here. I thought twice about doing you this favor since I wasn't sure if it was a favor at all. But I found that guy's chart and his address. I saw him three months ago so the address might still be helpful. Be careful old buddy. Look me up when you get a chance. I met a foxy little actress after you left last night so don't look me up tonight. I'll be busy." Bill then gave him the address of the man who had the tattoo. John jotted it down on a piece of hotel stationery, got dressed in jeans and stuffed the paper into his pocket. Before too long he was riding a series of trains in the graffiti ridden caverns of the New York subways that stank of electricity from the trains and urine from the homeless who hung out there. John got out of the subway system in the Village and then took a cab to the address he had in Chinatown.

"You sure you want to get out here, mister? This neighborhood ain't safe for you or anyone else. You ain't gonna get a cab too easily when you want to get out. How 'bout I take you to the Statue of Liberty for a little sight seeing?"

"No thanks. This is where I want to go."

The cabby took the money and tip and drove off. The neighborhood was a back alley of dingy tenements with laundry hanging off the fire escapes of some of the most run down brick buildings he had seen in the city. A few people milled around including some barefoot children in the street. They stared at him distrustfully only to look away quickly when he returned their gaze. 1423, apartment 3B. Slowly he went up to each building until he found the right one. Some stray cats nuzzled at his legs. The front doors were open. There was no buzzer to let someone in. With some reluctance he made his way up three flights of a narrow stairway until the plain white door of 3B, covered with dark smudges, stared at him in a completely uninviting way. The muffled sound of conversation came from behind the door. He knocked. No answer. He knocked again. The door swung open and a squat, round bellied Chinese man stood facing him with a look of surprise. The man's right hand clutched a can of beer. The smell of cooking grease and chicken greeted him.

"Hi. My name is John Bishop. I am very sorry to bother you but I could use your help."

The man looked at him with an uncomprehending expression.

John continued.

"I am looking for people who knew Wan Shin."

The flicker of recognition crossed the man's face followed by a cross expression. He walked into the apartment, and John followed him. About eight, mostly young Chinese men, some smoking, some drinking beer, sat scattered around a crowded living room of the small apartment. A TV blared, unnoticed, in a corner of the room. The man who had let John in said something loudly in Chinese followed by the name Wan Shin. The conversation stopped. There was a look of hostility on many of the men's faces. Finally, one of them, an older man, spoke.

"Nobody here knows any Wan Shin."

"I am sorry. But hospital records indicate that he lived in this apartment until he died a couple of months ago. Somebody must know of him. I would really like to talk with anyone who might know him."

"I live in this neighborhood 6 years. No Wan Shin."

Some of the men fidgeted nervously, and one of them went into a hallway to a phone on a table, quickly dialed a number and spoke rapidly in Chinese, gesturing, John thought, toward him on occasion.

"Well, perhaps you knew this man under a different name. If I told you the circumstances of his death perhaps then you would remember him. Several months ago the man was stabbed and then shot to death in the emergency room of the hospital. He had a tattoo, some kind of Chinese symbol on his right shoulder. Now, surely such an event would stand out in your minds."

Stoney silence. No one moved. No one spoke.

Finally the man who had shown him in took a gulp on his beer and spoke harshly to him. "Mister, you get out of here. You go now." The man shoved him awkwardly toward the door.

Reluctantly, John turned around and walked slowly out of the apartment. The look of recognition on the men's faces when he mentioned the name Wan Shin had given them away. Yet none of them dared say anything. Perhaps he had gone too far even in coming here. His footsteps echoed emptily as he descended the stairway.

Once in the street he looked around. No phone booth. With a smug sense of satisfaction at being able to counter a threatening situation he reached into his pocket and pulled out his cell phone and made his way briskly away from the building toward a main avenue. The cab company agreed to send a cab to meet him in ten minutes at the corner of his street and the main avenue two blocks away. Behind him a kid on bicycle was making his way toward him. Only ten or eleven years old, the kid yelled at him as he passed.

"You better run, mister. My brother's gonna catch you and beat you up. You musta done something bad."

The kid disappeared down a side street. Looking over his shoulder John saw ten or twelve young men, some with bats, running after him. John broke into a sprint and soon was sweating heavily under a warm autumn sun. The young Chinese men behind him were catching up to him quickly, and there remained perhaps four or five minutes before they would come close enough to grab him. Turning right onto the main avenue John noted some dumpsters to the side of a few stores. Lifting the lid of one he jumped inside landing in the midst of some foul smelling garbage. Nevertheless he pulled the lid over him, and the stench intensified. The street appeared to him through a thin crack, and soon the Chinese men burst into view looking everywhere for him. They split into groups going several different directions walking briskly and looking all around and even up fire escapes and at the upper stories of buildings.

His cab arrived. One of the men walked up to the cab, and after a few minutes the cab pulled away. Staring through the thin crack between the lid and the front of the garbage dump, trying not to breathe through his nose so he wouldn't gag on the stench, John watched as two men came straight for him. He felt around the garbage, wet and slimy in places, until he found a bottle, small comfort as a weapon for defense. The men stood directly in front of him, so close he thought he could even smell their sweat, see the threads in their white, stained T-shirts. Their voices were gruff and angry, and they pointed up, nodding and agreeing, it seemed, that their prey had fled through that particular fire escape to another street to safety and out of their grasp. From their slumped relaxed postures he could tell they had given up. One lit a cigarette and took deep inhalations of the smoke. All the talk was in Chinese except words in English that didn't have a direct translation. An address was being repeated. Hudson River dock. Tonight. He had the address. Yes it seemed like something was happening at that address which was some sort of shipping and receiving area off the river. One of them, to avoid hitting a passer-by in front of him, lifted the lid and John ducked down. The man had flicked his cigarette inside, and John brushed it off his arm, which stung from the burning ashes. The lid slammed down noisily and cautiously John rose up again and peered through his sliver of daylight. The men were walking away and soon had disappeared.

'I'm one lucky son of a bitch,' John thought and jumped out of the bin onto the street smiling broadly as a passersby looked at him oddly. John was so elated to be out of the garbage and away from the men that he wasn't bothered by the stares and looks of revulsion. 'They think I'm homeless,' he laughed to himself walking out to the street. No wonder that no cab would stop for him and in the subway people gave him ten feet of empty space.

Back in his hotel room John showered for a long time trying to get the repulsive stench of garbage out of his skin and hair. The doorman at the entrance of the hotel almost hadn't let him in. The poor man was quite appalled and confused. No matter. His room and the hot shower brought a sense of safety and comfort that he luxuriated in. Tonight would be a different situation. In the dead of night at the docks on the Hudson toward the lower end of Manhattan, he hoped to find some answers. Going alone, however, neither appealed to him nor made sense. Perhaps his friend Bill, the ER doc, would like to come along. Bill had a soft spot for adventure, perhaps even more so than women. He gave him a call.

"Hello, Bill? It's John."

" What's up?"

"How would you like to help me out tonight?"

"Sorry, buddy. You know I would if possible, but I'm going out with that actress I mentioned."

"Yeah, well, I visited that address you gave me and almost got my head bashed in. I overheard some talk about something happening at a dock on the Hudson at one am tonight. I think a shipment of some sort is coming in. I'd like to find out what is going on."

"It's probably drugs. I wouldn't get involved, buddy."

"Maybe. But if it's something else, there might be some kind of a lead for me."

Long pause.

"Ok. I'll cut my date short. I was hoping Carla would spend the night."

John smiled.

"Thanks. There'll be other times. Can you pick me up at 11?"

"11:30."

"I'll be waiting."

They hung up.

Later that night John and Bill were racing down Seventh Avenue to the lower west side of Manhattan in Bill's navy blue Miata. In the back seat lay a hodgepodge of tools and flashlights and small cameras that Bill had stuffed into a fanny pack.

"So what's the plan?" Bill said.

"Simple. We take a car and park near the address down there. Then we carefully come up to the place without anyone seeing us, poke around, gather some information and go. No one knows we came or went, and I will have some leads. These guys have no qualms about violence, so we've got to be extra careful."

"No. You don't have to warn me about that."

"I want as much information as we can get. Anything I can look into later. Addresses on boxes, copies of invoices, whatever. We can copy them down."

"Better yet we can photograph them. I brought a couple of small cameras."

"They'll work in the dark?"

"I do nature photography. Daytime, nighttime, in the forest, on the water, under the water. I have cameras for every occasion."

About thirty minutes later Bill parked his car on a dark and dirty street hedged by warehouses. They got out and Bill strapped on his fanny pack.

"Where to?" he whispered.

"Let's walk toward the river and try to find the address from there."

The river was soon visible dotted here and there by the lights of boats. Across the river parts of buildings and towers were lit up in New Jersey. The salt air invigorated them. The reflections of the lights, soft and silvery, danced on the water.

After a moment or two they were walking parallel to the river on a road that passed various shipping and receiving areas. Between the buildings the river would reappear enchantingly, moonlight streaked across its surface.

"I think we've got about a quarter of a mile to go," John said quietly.

"I know we wanted to park a discreet distance away, but perhaps we were a little too discreet," Bill answered.

The whole region was deserted.

"You sure you got the right night?" Bill said. "Doesn't look like much is happening."

"They were speaking Chinese. So, no, I'm not sure. But that doesn't matter. Look."

He pointed out in the river where a small ship was turning to come into a dock. The ship was about eighty feet long with a dark metal hull and a few lights in the cabins and was slowly turning in from the center of the river. Some men had gathered along the deck, ready with ropes to secure the ship to the dock.

"That's where we're going."

In five more minutes John stopped.

"This is it. We'll have to be really quiet. Look at all the cars parked out in front. There could be about twenty or thirty people here. Let's try to go around the back."

A wire mesh fence with barbwire on top surrounded the property. The door through the fence was unlocked, and they pushed it open just enough to get through. The gate let out a low creak nonetheless. Quickly they scooted to the side of the building, and reaching the back, they crouched down and stopped. Twenty men stood on the dock guiding the ship as it came in.

"Let's wait here for a minute and see what happens," John whispered directly into Bill's ear.

Bill slowly unzippered his fanny pack and pulled out some folding binoculars and peered through them at the ship. By now it was secured to the dock, and men from it were coming and talking to those waiting. The men on the dock were Chinese but those on the ship were European. Several wide planks were lowered to allow crew members to disembark. Some of the Chinese men walked over these and disappeared into the hold. Five minutes passed before the workers started coming out carrying medium and large sized boxes.

"Hey, pass those over to me." John stared through the binoculars and soon recognized several of the men he had seen in the apartment earlier that afternoon.

"Unloading could take a long time," John said. "Let's see if we can grab a box, open it up and put it back. Ok?"

Bill nodded, and they slowly crept toward the receiving bay, keeping low to the ground. There was a guard with a rifle slung over his shoulder and a pistol in a holster on a wide leather belt. His attention, though, was directed toward the ship. The two men, in a crouched down position, slowly made their way behind this man using the piles of rubble here and there as cover. From the back of a stack of wooden boxes, just in front of the warehouse entrance, John and Bill carefully watched the men coming and going and carrying and depositing the cardboard boxes toward the back of the storage area. On a piece of paper, John communicated his plan to Bill. At the right moment, both would dart to the back of the warehouse, pull one box into an adjacent room, examine the contents, put it back and then leave by the same route. The plan required perfect timing. It also required at least five more minutes of unloading.

Their opportunity came quickly. The warehouse lay empty and two men were making their way up the small climb with a particularly heavy box. John tugged at Bill's shoulder and the two ran quickly to the back where the boxes were stacked, grabbed a box and pulled it through a door into a side room. The sound of the two men breathing heavily and shoving a box around soon reached them. The echo of retreating footsteps resounded in the receiving area and then faded away. John cautiously peered around the doorframe and saw that the area was empty. The ship itself could not be seen from that angle but, nevertheless, now was the time to act. The two men set upon the box with ferocious intensity and ripped it open.

"Incredible," Bill said.

"Biolab equipment," John responded.

"More than that. I've seen this before in the genetics lab at the university. Most of this stuff is out of my scope."

"Look," John said. "Here is a label. Have you heard of this place? It's in New York State. It's a community hospital."

Bill stared at the address for a minute.

"Yeah, as a matter of fact I have. It's in the northern part of Westchester County."

"Why the hell is it going there?"

"Who knows? I'll photograph the label and some of the contents and then we need to get our butts out of here."

From his fanny pack Bill pulled out a small camera, but neither man, in their fascination, for what they had found noticed the soft footsteps of a man coming toward them. One of the workers had to use the bathroom and had returned by himself. Walking toward the back of the receiving area, he saw a flash of light come from the room where John and Bill crouched. The man looked into the room, saw the two strange men and screamed and turned around to run back to the ship to warn the others.

Quickly the doctors slid the box back and saw that the entire crew of workers was racing up the small embankment toward them effectively blocking the route by which they had come. Reluctantly, the two of them fled into the building running past a few startled men sipping coffee and smoking cigarettes. They landed in a room that looked out onto the front of the property and slid the window open and jumped out slamming the window shut behind them. The workers burst into the room looked around and then ran out giving the two fugitives about thirty seconds to get through the front gate and into the road. The workers were soon behind them fanning into different directions. Some headed for their cars. John and Bill took a winding route of back alleys, crouching low, as the yells and shouts of their pursuers pierced the air, and then, finally, they were able to jump into the Miata and turn with tires screeching and wailing back toward the avenues that would lead them toward the upper west side.

"I think we lost them," Bill yelled over the roar of the wind passing over the convertible.

"Maybe," John said. He looked behind them searching the traffic for signs of one of the cars. "I think I saw one of them following us. A white chevy. I don't see it now. Be careful when you go home. Make sure none of these guys see where you live. Secure your doors with every lock you've got."

"Don't worry about me. I've got fifteen years of karate and a black belt so a bunch of puny gangsters aren't going to intimidate me."

"If they come after you with guns they won't look so puny anymore."

Bill laughed.

"I got into karate to protect myself from the city and from God-knows-who that will enter the ER when I'm working. Basically it's self-delusion as all these gangbangers carry some pretty heavy artillery. I'm used to watching my back, though, so don't lose any sleep on my account. Here's your hotel. When I get the film developed I'll give you a call. This got more interesting than I expected which for an adventure junky like me is great. So, see ya tomorrow, buddy. "

John got out and watched as Bill pulled back into traffic. He scoured the traffic for any signs of the men that had pursued them from the dock. Only an anonymous stream of cars weaved and honked and raced noisily by. John walked back into the hotel, went up to his room and quickly went to bed and fell asleep.

Chapter XII

The following morning he called Bill. The phone rang and rang. Finally someone answered.

"Hello, Bill?"

A female voice responded.

"This is Carla. Bill isn't feeling too well right now."

"Well, this is really important. I have to talk to him, even if only for a second. What, does he have the flu? A fever?"

"No. It's not the flu. He got mugged."

"Oh." Guilt knotted up in his chest. " Sorry to hear that. Could you tell him John Bishop is calling?"

"John Bishop?"

At this point Bill grabbed the phone and spoke in a hoarse, pained and weary voice.

"John, I'm out. I can't afford to get involved in this stuff. I've got a 24-hour shift in the ER tonight and I don't know how I'm going to make it. I think they fractured my jaw."

"Oh, my God. I'm sorry. Bill, just tell me, what happened?"

"They came last night. They must have followed me home."

"The Chinamen?"

"Well, they weren't all Chinese. Some were American. Some were central or South American. There were six of them. Frankly they immobilized me pretty fast."

"Did they have guns?"

"I thought so. I couldn't be sure. I didn't fight back for that reason."

"Out of fear that they had a gun?"

"Right. Well, they wanted the film. They just asked me at first. I pretended ignorance. This just infuriated them. They began kicking me. Some of my ribs must be broken. They're awfully sore. Finally, along with my ribs, I caved in. I gave them the film."

"So they left."

"Not right away. One of the bigger guys came over and beat me up pretty badly. He was such a sadist. I could see he was smiling. My jaw doesn't open right because of that bastard. I plan to get an x-ray tonight."

"I'm awfully sorry, Bill. It should've been me."

"Don't worry about it. It's not your fault. I knew what could happen. I consider myself lucky to be alive. Just one thing."

"What?"

"Next time you've got one of these adventures, do me a favor."

"Anything."

"Count me out. In fact don't even mention it to me. I might forget how much pain I'm in right now and get tempted to try this again. I am not trying to put a guilt trip on you, buddy. I hope you get those bastards, but I've got a life here in New York I've got to take care of. " Bill hung up.

Poor guy got more than he expected, and in a way John could not blame him for being angry. Bill would get over it but clearly the man could not help him from now on. Adventure is one thing, but the loss of a hard-won career or even death meant something else altogether. John felt the same way, but for him the choice lay between danger and destruction, a slim hope and none.

He picked up the phone again and dialed Gabby's number at home.

"Hello?" came the laconic reply, her voice full of that low, sleep-deprived timbre.

"Gabby. This is John."

"That's nice. Don't you think it's a bit early to be calling on a Saturday?"

"It's 10 in the morning. Late by your standards. I always remember you as getting up early and bustling around with an ungodly amount of energy and cheerfulness."

"Very funny. Not so loud. I've got a headache." There was a pause and then she spoke very quietly. "Jack is here."

"Well, this is important."

"Okay. But make it quick. Jack is going to wake up, soon."

"Fine. I went to Morgan, Morgan and Associate."

"I know all about that. A preliminary report has already come."

"That sure is fast. How did you find out about it?"

"Somebody from them called us to let us know that is was ready and that she would be coming down to give us their findings. I think her name was Stacey Simmons."

The name came like a punch to his solar plexus.

"Are you sure that's her name?"

"I'm pretty sure. Her picture was with her resume. Blond, attractive. Did you meet her up there?"

"You could say so."

"She's pretty engaging, don't you think so?"

"No. Not really."

"What?"

"Never mind. She's not important. Just a messenger. Just a goddamn messenger."

For a moment his mind felt numb and cold. After a pause he forced himself to continue.

"Well, anyway this is not about that company. I want to tell you what happened after my meeting there."

John then related the events involving the Chinamen and the dock.

"Mr. Curiosity always getting in trouble. When will you ever learn?"

"It's a two-edged sword. This time is brought some rewards."

"Well, I've got something for you, too."

"What is that?"

"I can't tell you now. You need to get here as soon as you can. Pronto. I'll meet you at your place in six hours or less. That should be enough time."

"No clues?"

"Not a one. I'll tell you the story when I see you. Call me as soon as you arrive. One suggestion, though. Pick up some sun block. You're going to need a lot where you are going. Shorts and a hat would work, too." She hung up.

'Silly woman,' he thought. She always liked to tease and torment me. Nevertheless he had his bags packed in minutes and before long was cruising down the interstate back to Maryland.

Chapter XIII

After arriving home, while unpacking in his bedroom, he heard his phone ring. He picked it up.

"Hello?"

"Oh, good, John, you're here," Gabby sighed.

"That's right and I am ready for you to tell me where this sunny place is. If you remember I happen to like sunny places."

"Of course I remember. The Caribbean. St. Martin. How's that?"

"Wow. If I weren't so stressed out I might enjoy this. What's the big deal with St. Martin?"

"I'll tell you when I see you."

"OK. How about in five days?"

"How about in five minutes?"

"Is this type A behavior going on here or am I in really big trouble."

"Probably both. A big lead has popped up. I'll tell you when I see you. As it stands now in three hours you will be leaving on a flight from Baltimore. That gives you time to repack and for me to come over and give you your tickets and reservations in St. Martin and to tell you a little about what is going on."

"Now, you're really scaring me, Gabby."

"I don't mean to. But, yes, it is serious. Interesting and serious."

"Ok. Sun block, shorts and a hat are ready. I am trusting you that this is important for me to do this."

"It is. See you shortly. Don't forget your passport."

Barely five minutes later Gabby pulled into his driveway and let herself into his house.

Her smile appeared forced. As John finished packing, Gabby delivered her explanation.

"The hospital is getting stranger and stranger. For example I thought I had Ed Brogan, the CEO pegged, but all of a sudden my impressions of him are changing completely. Do you know him?"

"I know who he is. I think he greeted me once at a reception for one of the more important physician practices for the hospital. You know. That one for the new orthopedic clinic."

"Yes. He's particularly fond of our orthopods. Well, I deal with him all the time. His usual behavior is sort of friendly, outgoing but also rather domineering. He's in charge. But then again he's the boss. So taking charge and controlling the situation is rather expected. Brogan is the pillar of the community, on the board of country clubs, cultural organizations including philanthropic ones."

"The ideal citizen, right?"

"Well, I never thought he was very sincere. Sort of a social climber. All of a sudden he isn't so friendly to me anymore. In fact he's been downright hostile. He snaps at me. I can't do anything right or do it fast enough. He started dropping little hints that he might know I was helping you and that he didn't appreciate that and that if I knew what was right for my career I should stop it. He didn't come out and say these things of course but it wasn't too hard to guess."

"I am not quite sure how he knows that you are helping me, but I guess a man with his power has some connections and sources on the grapevine."

"Exactly. Just be careful who you talk to. Like Morgan, Morgan and Associates. They talk to you and he talks to them. He or the hospital is paying the tab. But since he signs the check he gets to see everything."

"I was originally happy with that company, but now I regret ever having spilled my guts to them."

"Absolutely. That's not why I came here though. There's been a break in the information I have about Eva Bentley."

"Great!"

"Okay. Quite simply Eva Bentley made a lot of trips to the Caribbean in addition to her other travels. Almost all of them were to St. Martin. A few were to St. Vincent but not that many. The obvious question is why? You're going down to help figure this out."

"How did you find out about this?"

"Purely by accident. David had asked Morgan, Morgan and Associates for a rundown of Eva's activities for the past two years. The company called Brogan for a confirmation of this request. Brogan confirmed the request but insisted that the report would be reviewed by him only. In other words no one was to read it except him. Well, normally all fiscal reports coming to Ed Brogan come to me first so I can condense them for him due to his time limitations. Well, the report from Morgan, Morgan and Associates had the appearance of a fiscal report because the company tracked her comings and goings mainly through financial transactions. Brogan's secretary misread the nature of the report and sent it to me. I went through just a few pages and realized a mistake had been made but thought oh what the hell and read the whole thing. It was pretty damn interesting. I sent it right back to his secretary and pretended I hadn't looked at it."

"Did you get a copy?"

"Do I look stupid?"

"Just checking. Where is it?"

"At home. Nothing in my office is really safe from Brogan. Not really."

"Tell me about the trips."

"Every 4 to 6 weeks she would fly down to St. Martin, and as I said occasionally St. Vincent. After four or five days she would come back."

"Where did she stay?"

"La Grace. A very fancy French resort. You're going to like it"

She reached into her pocket book and gave him airline tickets and his reservations for La Grace.

"You leave tomorrow morning at 8:20. You can pay me back later."

"What's the rush on this?"

"I think Brogan wants to dump the whole situation on you and that would pretty much bring you down completely unless you can get more information."

"We're back to that, huh?"

"We're back to that."

"What do I do when I get there?"

"Take this photo of Eva. Ask questions. Try to get some idea of her activities down there. Get names of associates. A beautiful woman who visits the same place so often is bound to be remembered by a lot of different people."

"What about arousing suspicions?

"Make up a story. You could say she was a cousin or friend and you are just reminiscing about her. Also, you won't be staying down there for long and don't try to extend your stay no matter how beautiful it is. Jack and I are going down toward the end of your visit. We'll be staying at La Grace, too, but we won't be asking any questions about anything. For us this is strictly vacation. However, should things begin to go badly for you and you need our help, we'll be there. Otherwise we shouldn't talk at all. Pretend to be strangers. OK?"

"Got it."

"Any questions?"

"Just hundreds."

"Save them until you get back. We'll have a breakfast meeting."

"How are the legal proceedings going?"

"Cannon shots on both sides. Things are heating up. I wish I had better news. Fortunately you have the Caribbean to mellow you out before you face all that. Pina coladas, topless women, white sand beaches. At least on this trip there is a brighter side."

"Relaxation would help."

"Don't get distracted down there. But there is no harm in enjoying yourself. I get the feeling there is some good information that could open things up. Well, I have to go. I'll walk myself to the door. Be careful, John."

"Bye, Gabby."

She walked out the front door and minutes later her black BMW screeched out of the driveway. For one forlorn minute he stared after her and then resumed packing.

The next morning he sat packed into the coach section of a passenger jet roaring its way to the Caribbean. The plane touched down briefly in Miami and then resumed its journey to St. Martin. After it had landed John walked down the stairs onto the tarmac and stared into the bright sunshine, which greeted him with overpowering heat and humidity. He loved the weather.

Passage through the airport was uneventful, and soon his small rental car had him careening through the streets of the island toward La Grace. A mile or two into his journey he noticed a jeep keeping pace with his car. Hungary all over again. He looked into his rearview mirror. The jeep was gone. Then from around a curve there the black jeep reappeared. His course took him down a deserted dusty road bordered by rolling brown hills covered with cactus on one side, and on the other side vistas of the sea. Speckled with whitecaps and waves that crashed upon deserted beaches, the Caribbean spread out before him. A small, white sign marked the turn to La Grace on a road that ran between two of the hills. After he went over the ridge, the barrenness of the hills yielded to the luxurious splendor of the resort. The buildings, meticulously tended, were painted in yellows and pinks and blues. Gardens of brilliantly colored flowers surrounded many of the buildings. A cove opened into a marina full of motorboats, sailboats and white yachts, some over a hundred feet long.

After parking he strolled into the lobby to the receptionist's desk but kept his eye on the parking lot where in minutes the black jeep pulled up and stopped. A muscular, young man with a scraggly beard and sunglasses and wearing a dirty T-shirt, shorts and sandals got out and leaned against the Jeep staring in John's direction. After a few minutes the man got back into the rusting, dented vehicle and drove away.

"May I help you?" the woman at the front desk said displaying a broad smile of white teeth.

"Yes. John Bishop. Checking in."

Carrying his bags the porter soon guided him through the compound of villas, rooms, swimming pools, restaurants and bars and extensive sports facilities all forming the famous and pricey French resort known as La Grace. After the porter left, John stared out of his window, which gave him a view of the marina. He unpacked, donned shorts, polo shirt and sandals and left his room in search of the beach.

A narrow wooden walkway led through the sand and dunes to the sea beyond, and John quickly joined the mothers and fathers and children walking with towels and beach toys towards La Plage. Most of the people around him spoke French although Americans and Germans also were present.

Once walking in the sand he took off his sandals and looked around. The beach was sparsely populated. Attractive women sunbathed serene and topless on beach chairs and towels. Children played in the easy surf. In the distance larger waves crashed against a reef. From the tropical sun the water lit up in clear and bluish brilliance revealing the bright white sand at the bottom. To his left was a beach bar covered with a thatched roof and he headed over and quickly secured a cold pina colada dripping perspiration. As he settled under an umbrella sipping the cool, delicious drink surrounded by Caribbean beauty the thought came to him that he should never leave.

The alcohol, like some invisible hypnotist, soon caused his mind to numb and his legs and arms to just let go. He closed his eyes and all he had was the sound of the surf rhythmically sweeping his mind clear, pulling him into a thoughtful reverence for the force of nature. Strangely enough as he fell deeper into his own self, he found the difficult knot of the mystery of Eva Bentley tense and unyielding and defying him to unravel its tenacious character.

His eyes opened, and now the Caribbean scene seemed just out of reach like a commercial beckoning one to a vacation that one could not afford. Slowly, stiffly and perhaps mournfully he got up and went back over to the dive shop. Air tanks and equipment lay everywhere. There was brand new equipment for sale and lots of rental equipment, which looked much less glamorous. Many tanks lay all over the floor in an adjoining room waiting to be filled up with compressed air again. Several young men, athletic and tanned, hung around waiting for customers or doing various chores. One of them, blond and muscular came up to John.

"Can I help you?"

"Yes, I'm down here for a vacation and would like to do a little scuba diving but have never done it. Is there anything I could sign up for to get started?"

"Sure. We have lessons every day. How long are you down for?"

"About a week."

"Why don't you come to tomorrow's late afternoon class? It starts at 3:30 and lasts for two and a half hours. It's in English. We offer courses in French, English and sometimes German. After that you'll be able to do some of the simple dives around the island. Some of the dive sites just off shore have wrecks at 30 feet. We give you a beginner's certificate and that'll let you rent equipment just about anywhere around here."

"Sounds exciting. What do I do?"

"Just sign up on this sheet and be at the main pool in your bathing suit at 3:30. We provide all the equipment."

"I'll be there."

John scribbled his name below a list of about 20 others and then left the dive shop. Despite himself his excitement soared over the prospects of this colorful pastime. With stubborn, childish desire, he planned to steal part of an afternoon to explore the dazzling beauty of a tropical reef. Right now lay the task of prodding employee memories for information on Eva.

A maid pushed her cart toward the guest rooms.

"Excuse me, Ma'am. Have you ever seen this woman?"

The woman took the photograph from his hands and within seconds handed it back to him.

"Alors, monsieur, no one here remembers that woman. Personne!" she said muttering angrily to herself and continued pushing her cart without looking back at John.

In the gift shop the saleslady politely approached him.

"May I help you, sir?"

"Yes, you can. Have you worked at the resort for very long?"

"Three years."

"Good. Ever see this woman?"

The woman's smile faded, and she handed the photograph back to him.

"Sorry, sir, maybe the receptionist could help you," and immediately the woman turned away to help another customer.

The maid was right. Nobody remembered seeing her. Yet everybody's reactions told him they had.

The next day John sat patiently dangling his legs in the pool waiting with the rest of the guests for the dive class to start. The instructor, a tall man in his thirties with dark hair and the sleek body of a swimmer, arrived. He wore a white T-shirt.

"OK, folks," he began. "We're starting. Everybody gather around. This is a beginner's scuba class so you are going to learn the basics. After you complete the course you'll be able to do open ocean dives down to thirty feet. There will be more advanced classes as the week goes on. Raise your hands if you are doing this for the first time."

Everyone but one couple raised their hands.

"Good. Let's get started then. We're going to first give out the equipment and go over what each piece is used for."

The lessons proceeded. Towards the end of the class John had gathered enough confidence to sit at the bottom of the pool drawing air from his tank or to calmly swim around enjoying the ease afforded by his own portable air supply. The instructor, still wearing his T-shirt swam over to him and nudged him to come up and together they burst through the surface.

"Don't get into a trance down there. If you lose your air at 70 feet you could have a lot of trouble getting back to the surface."

Instead of responding John noticed a dark tatoo on the man's right shoulder that was showing through the wet T-shirt. Part of the tatoo looked like waves. They stared at each other for a minute, and then the instructor abruptly swam away.

"Ok, everybody. It's time to wrap things up. Put your equipment in the appropriate piles. I've got a few things to tell you, and then you can go."

A short time later everyone had completed their tasks and sat waiting by the pool, tired and exhilarated over their new experiences and newly acquired skills.

"Congratulations. You have all completed this beginner's course successfully," the instructor said smiling. "Tomorrow, after the dive shop opens at 8 in the morning, you can pick up your certificate which allows you to dive at any of the easiest dives on the island designated by a diamond on the dive map. You are also eligible for some of the more advanced classes such as night diving and wreck diving. When you pick up your card you can sign up for these classes if you want. Thank you. You've been a wonderful group."

As everyone else left, John walked over to the instructor who looked up at him expectantly.

"Do you need something, John?" he said.

"Perhaps just some information. I have a friend who used to come down here all the time, and I have been trying to locate her. I was wondering if you know anything about her or where I might find her."

"Maybe. What's her name?"

"Eva Bentley."

The smile ebbed from the instructor's face. He looked down at the ground.

"Never heard of her. Sorry, John. We have lots of guests who come here. Some I remember some I don't."

"I know it's hard because you see so many people, but before you decide you never met her, let me show you her picture."

John dug it out of his pack and handed it over to the instructor. The man took it and studied it for a brief moment before handing it back .The man's face grew taut.

"Doesn't ring a bell. I suggest you try one of the other resorts."

"Ok. Well, time for dinner. Thanks for a good class." John turned around and slowly walked toward his room, and felt the eyes of the instructor staring into his back. When he was rounding a turn in the sidewalk he glanced over to the pool. The instructor was gone. All the equipment lay abandoned in heaps by the pool.

After John had showered and then dressed for dinner, he stepped outside once again to go to one of the restaurants to eat. A brilliant, Caribbean sunset spread across the sky. Bright oranges and reds flared amidst the cooler blues and purples, and the ocean, through innumerable shimmering reflections, shared in the glorious rush of colors. In the restaurant a man from his scuba course motioned him over to his table.

"Hi. You look a little lost. Have a seat. Why don't you have dinner with me? Ed Piercely. I'm from Long Island." The man extended his hand, and John shook it and reluctantly sat down.

"John Bishop."

"I come down here once a year usually with one of my buddies, but this year none of them could make it. They're all getting married. Not me. I don't really go for all this palm tree crap and Caribbean magic. I come here for only two things. The rum and the babes. Especially the ones on the beach, if you know what I mean. Usually I get lucky with one of the French babes. They think a guy from Long Island is pretty exotic."

And so the dinner went. After the conch soup and shrimp appetizer John found the courage to say goodbye to his new friend.

"I'd better get to the bathroom. Bad seafood yesterday. Thanks for sharing your table with me, Ed."

"You got the revenge, huh? I know what you mean, dude. Got it myself last year. I'll save a babe for you at the bar. See ya there, buddy."

John exited the restaurant. In the damp but invigorating ocean air outside he savored his freedom. The resort provided entertainment nearly every night in the courtyard where there were tables and chairs and an outdoor bar and torches lit all around. John walked over to this area and took a seat at the bar. A canopy of stars graced the night sky. Somehow having the ocean nearby in every direction enhanced his sense of romance and adventure.

"Drink, sir?" the bartender intoned.

"Sure. Pina Colada."

John watched as the bartender went about making the drink. The muscular man worked with flawless precision and speed before producing the icy drink with its colorful fruit adorning the glass. From his pocket John pulled out the photo of Eva Bentley, and studied her features. Her hair fell in shimmering, sultry beauty across her shoulder. Her eyes sparkled with life and yet at the same time held sadness. Would he have liked her had he known her better?

"Your drink, sir. Should I run up a tab?"

"Yeah, that would be great. By the way. Every see this lady?"

John handed the picture to the bartender who took it, glanced at it and handed it back. The bartender was silent.

"Cat got your tongue."

"No, sir."

"Well, what do you think?"

"She been here. Many times."

"Do you know anything about her?"

"Enough to stay away. She trouble, mon."

"What did she do down here?

"She liked to scuba, mon."

"Any favorite spots?"

"Pig Island. She never go anywhere else. Don't go there, mon. They found a tourist in the surf across from Pig Island, dead. They think he was buying drugs."

The bartender slipped away for more guests were milling in from the restaurants to get ready for the show. He was quickly very busy filling drink orders. Too bad. The man had more information and seemed to have been willing to talk.

John sipped his drink and began to relax. Torches around the courtyard flickered and left their black, smoky trail. The rumble of the surf came from over the dunes. The tables filled up quickly with guests dressed casually, smiling and talking in lighthearted ways. People that came late stood in clusters. There was an air of anticipation. A calypso band played a few tunes and then abruptly stopped when a smiling black man came up to the microphone looking out over a crowd that quickly hushed.

"Ladies and Gentlemen," he said pausing. "Welcome. Welcome. Our program tonight is a very special one. There is a tradition that came to our island from ancient traditions of Africa. Here is the Mocko Jumbie! Please welcome our Mocko Jumbie dancer tonight. I am sure you will be enchanted."

There was polite applause.

"Our second performer will delight you as well. He is a glass walker who will do amazing things on broken glass with only his bare skin to protect him. He will also invite members of the audience to participate in some of his tricks. So beware. Beware. He may call upon you. Now the first performance will begin."

The man walked away from the microphone, and the band started up a very rhythmic type of music with a strong and complex percussion. The crowd waited expectantly for several minutes when from around the corner the Mocko Jumbie appeared. Dressed in a silk white suit the dancer rose high above the ground on stilts. White gloves covered the hands and a mask all white with black, cat-like markings, covered the face. The movements were focused and intense and very quickly the dancer had wrapped the crowd in a shroud of magic springing forth from the mysticism of ancient tribal traditions from the plains and jungles of Africa. One by one people from the crowd got up and went over to the Mocko Jumbie to hand him a dollar, which was accepted with a short, polite ritual that ended with a handshake. John reached into his wallet and soon found himself on the dance floor reaching way up to deliver the token to the mysterious dancer. He shook hands against the soft white glove and stared into the masked face and then left but not before noticing that directly beyond his scuba instructor had gotten up hastily from a table and left the courtyard.

John decided to follow the man and walked quickly after him so as not to lose sight of him. The instructor hurried toward the dive shop, which was dark except for a window in the back that glowed dimly with a yellow light. Just as the instructor reached the building, an older man came out to greet him. John crept up to the men as close as he could get and hid behind a shed. His tennis shoes made little noise that, in any case, became lost in the sounds of the surf coming from over the dunes. The conversation was hushed but discernible.

"There is someone asking about Eva," the instructor said.

"Who is that?"

"Some guy named John. He was in my scuba class today."

"What's he want?"

"Information. I don't know what exactly. I pretended not to know anything about her."

"That may have been a stupid idea. Why's he askin?"

"I don't know."

"Where is he now?"

"Back at the bar."

"Good. I'd better call the boss on this one."

Together they disappeared into the dive shop. John tried to listen under the window but couldn't hear anything. Reluctantly he left, but instead of going back to his room walked over the dunes to the beach and sat down on one of the chairs. The full moon splashed a silver streak across the dark, calm ocean. The lights of a few ships winked in the distance. Tall palm trees stood as silent sentinels. Tomorrow morning, first thing, he would have to go to Eva's island before those men could stop him or knew what he was up to.

The rain fell more heavily now, and the drops splashed noisily on the stone of the square. As his head was thrust brusquely down onto the block he could still see the blood of those who had preceded him. The faces around him looked on impassively. There was horror, but compassion did not appear among them. Thunder rolled noisily in the distance. A hood was thrust over his head and the outside world gave way to darkness. He wondered how much pain he would feel. Beside him the executioner awaited a nod from the King who, eager to have these events finished, quickly assented. The huge man seized the ax and slowly raised it over his head. Lightning flashed in the background. The crowd was beginning to stir. The storm was frightening them. To leave now would be a capital offense to the King, and no one dared move.

Chapter XIV

The next morning the alarm from the clock radio on the bed table buzzed obnoxiously. 6:30 am. Reluctantly John rose from the comfort of his bed to get dressed to go to the dive shop. Outside the already hot and humid air contrasted with the air-conditioned coolness of his room. An hour after awakening he was tentatively pulling open the door to the dive shop. His entrance, a half-hour before opening time, caused suspicious glances to fall on him from the workers. At the desk one of them asked to help him.

"John Bishop. Here to get my certificate from yesterday's beginner's course."

The muscular young guy looked down his list.

"I see you're eager to get started. Ok. Just sign here," and slipped a card to John.

"Thanks."

"Are you diving this morning?"

"Nope."

"Care to join one of ours? There's still room on the ten o'clock for the old Navy wreck."

"Thanks. Maybe tomorrow."

"Need any help with your plans to see the island?"

"No thanks," and John pulled away from the desk and the overzealous helpfulness of the young man.

John left with the imprint of the suspicious glances firmly in his mind. Aside from him only the workers milled around in the shop getting ready for the various dives and classes for the day. His plan rushed to mind. Leave immediately for Pig Island and pick up dive equipment and a bathing suit along the way. Don't give anyone a chance to perceive or interfere with his plans. Always with him, his passport and wallet lay in his pockets.

He passed through the lobby and then into the parking lot. As he pulled out in his rental car he glanced all around for signs of anyone following him or watching him. No one anywhere gave him that impression. Before long his car was weaving its way down the winding ribbon of a road that followed the ocean off to his right. The water glimmered in bright blue and, for the moment, gave him some measure of peace.

Ten minutes into his journey he came to a hotel on the water with a pool into which ocean waves crashed. Beyond that was a beach and a dive shop on the other side of the road. Beginner diving classes were getting started on the beach. After parking he entered the shop and twenty minutes later came out laden with some well-worn equipment, a new bathing suit and admonishments from the salesmen to stick to well-marked, easy dive sites, which a map indicated very clearly.

With a lurch his car was off again, and the road now ran away from the ocean into the countryside. Green pastures and rolling hills lay all around. A young man, shirtless with dreadlocks, on a stripped down motorcycle, went roaring past him without a helmet. Soon the road started to veer back toward the ocean, and John began to look for the turn. It was an unmarked dirt road that led to an unused beach, the water and then Pig Island.

The turn was across from a local bar and grocery store, two tumbledown, concrete buildings with iron bars on the front doors and windows. He turned to the right and the road quickly became so rough he had to slow down as the car bounced and jarred through the potholes. Finally the view in front opened up to the ocean and the foliage around him began to thin out. The road started to turn sandy so John pulled to the side and parked before getting stuck in the softer sand up ahead. Some trees remained to hide his car.

After changing into his bathing suit and hiding his clothes, passport and wallet in the car, he quickly dragged his equipment down to the surf and gazed out before him. Straight across from him, about a few hundred yards away, stood Pig Island. On the French maps it was Le Cochon. Full of scraggly brush and rocks and clusters of trees here and there the island hardly seemed interesting, and yet for Eva Bentley it was almost an obsession.

John pulled on his gear and then waded awkwardly through the small waves before plunging into the water. The air from the tank had to be saved for exploration around the island. His snorkel allowed him to gaze under water at the sand and coral and multicolored tropical fish. Blue fish with white stripes, red fish with yellow fins and yellow ones shaped liked flattened pancakes all swam before him with carefree nonchalance. A five-foot barracuda, motionless except for its pectoral fins, stared at him from twenty feet away. A stonefish with spiky lateral fins and brown and white stripes lumbered lazily along the sandy bottom. The fascination of the underwater display made the trip across the channel pass quickly.

When he came within fifty feet of the island he raised his head out of the water and studied the shoreline of the island. To the right a cliff of rock dropped around fifty feet to the surface of the ocean. His first exploration would start there where his presence would be inconspicuous.

After coming even closer he placed the regulator into his mouth and then plunged down toward the bottom before leveling off and coursing straight for the rock face of the cliff. At first, just a dark smudge on the rock and then a more distinct rectangle made clear evidence of a human device. At ten feet the dark rectangle was clearly a metal door of some sort with a hinge on top and a lock down below. John tried to pull on the handle but the lock held fast. He took out his diving knife and tried to pry open the door but failed to budge it. The bolt in the hinge from use and corrosion had a little play in it. John dove to the bottom where tiny reef fish darted away, picked up a rock and then inserted the blade of the knife against the head of the bolt. He banged the rock against the top of the knife until finally the bolt broke free and, with a little more work, fell out allowing the heavy door to be pulled open against the lock below. Beyond the door was a tunnel big enough for a man to swim through. Taking his flashlight from his belt, John slipped beyond the door into the tunnel as the beam of his light pierced the inky, lifeless darkness in the tunnel. The air gauge for his tank revealed a remaining pressure of only half his starting amount.

The tunnel, which was actually a rough natural cave, gradually sloped upwards as John swam warily forward alert to any offshoots that would confuse his return to the open ocean. None were found, and no detectable life swam the waters of the tunnel. About fifty yards into it, his beam illuminated a cement step. John swam over and soon was climbing up about ten steps of a staircase that led from the water through a rounded pool into a large vaulted cavern deep inside the island. His mind registered shock at the sight of hundreds of tiny lights, green, red, blue and white, flickering and burning back at him from equipment and technology that packed the cavern and hummed with the flow of electricity.

He swung his flashlight around the room. The array of electronics and other sophisticated technology stirred no recognition except for the occasional computer. Dripping ocean water he climbed out of the pool and took off his scuba gear so he could explore the room unhindered. Where was a light switch? There, on a back wall his flashlight beam illuminated a switch. He flipped it on and then several others and the room lit up. Within a large, natural cavern of black, craggy rock stood a stunning compound of technology.

Eva came here. He felt this with a sure knowledge and could almost feel her presence – the beautiful young woman with the dazzling smile and that penetrating intelligence that held in some dark corner a ruthlessness that baffled him. What had she been doing here? The answers lay before him and somehow he had to decode the significance of this cavern and its technological treasure. He beheld a modern day pirate's cave with some new kind of gold and silver. Gauging by the expense of the equipment this pirate operation must be bringing in a large quantity of money.

While John lumbered slowly around the cavern fascinated by his discovery, miles away on the main island an alarm had gone off. A dark haired man looked up from his newspaper at some meters that were registering an unexpected increase in current. He tapped at his computer and plugged in readings from the meters and quickly determined the location where the surge in electrical use was occurring. Then he brought up the schedule for that location. Empty. No one was supposed to be there. Concern mounted within him, and he picked up the phone and dialed a long distance number. The event was too important to be handled locally. Watching the dials the man spoke hastily.

"Jefe. Hay un problema.... Si. Pig Island...Hay un pinche cabron en la cueva... Sorry, boss. Si, English. Sombody is in the cave in Pig Island. Better get someone over, pronto...No. I don't know how many, but I suggest you send four or five hombres with guns right away."

After assuring himself that no one was around and that no cameras surveyed the open space, John relaxed and studied the room while moving from one piece of equipment to the other. The place fascinated him. Although the technology baffled him, he could tell it had a biomedical purpose. Some of it reminded him of various research labs he had spent time in between his first and second year of medical school. The file cabinets were locked. PC's perched on top of desks, but no loose papers lay around and the computers abruptly blocked any attempts at accessing files by demanding a password.

Furthest from the entry pool appeared an area of bins and drawers that would pull out if not locked and that had digital readouts of temperature and various other parameters. Clearly the bins, vaults and drawers stored something, probably whatever was the main purpose of the cavern, the gold that it guarded. He took out his underwater camera and photographed the area extensively. The locks to each of the storage points had a numerical code to unlock it. Punching in random numbers yielded nothing.

John sat staring and thinking.

Finally an idea occurred to him. He stretched his memory as hard as he could to remember Eva Bentley's birth date. Her chart slowly came into mental focus. She was 27 years old. April. April 14. He punched in the numbers on a vault. Nothing. Systematically he went through the different ones. Halfway through one of the bins hummed and whirred and slowly opened up yielding white condensation as the cold interior met the damp air. Inside was a small, metal square box with a handle that he pulled out with part of his wet suit to protect himself from the cold.

He took the box to one of the tables near the entry pool and prepared to try and open it. Abruptly the lights went off, and the room plunged into darkness. Stunned he tried to get his bearings. The pool lay less than ten feet away, and beside it, in a heap along with his flashlight, rested his scuba gear. The thought struck him with a cold shock that somehow his presence here had tripped a security system. His body snapped alive. He listened quietly. The gentle lapping of the pool, reflections of the ocean activity outside, came to him from his left. Stuffing the metal box into a fanny pack, he slowly edged himself in the direction of the pool, reaching out with his feet to try and lightly touch a piece of his equipment.

His foot brushed an object.

Reaching down he pulled up his mask and with relief began quickly putting on his gear. His hasty actions caused something to start rolling toward the pool. His flashlight! He stretched out his hand only to brush the rubberized cylinder of the flashlight and cause it to roll even faster. A dull splash raised the bitter awareness that the flashlight had fallen into the water and now laid among the rocks and crevices on the bottom.

His stomach muscles tightened into a chaotic array of knots. Somewhere down on the irregular rocky bottom of the pool, lay his flashlight. He took a few deep breaths to settle his thoughts and then put on his scuba equipment taking painstaking care not to repeat his very costly mistake. He descended down the cement steps into the utter darkness of the water orienting his course to the opening of the tunnel leading out to sea from the position of the steps and the lights behind him.

Under water any sense of orientation quickly left him. There was no up, down or forward or backward - only the unyielding darkness. Once he pushed off from the stairs, he had to feel his way around the rocks and before finding the tunnel that he entered. Disorientation and dread filled his senses. The darkness encased him. His hands reached down to pull himself along the bottom. Only the rough and sometimes slippery sensations of the rocks upon his hands curbed a panic that threatened to paralyze his mind. His head bumped into a wall. His hands crawled up it and touched metal. Peering carefully, he could see specks of light where the door stood slightly ajar from the edge. Someone had replaced it while he was gone.

A thought struck him with cold fear.

The door had been fixed from outside.

Probably ten minutes of air remained in his tank. His air gauge was unreadable without his flashlight. The tension hung like a cold stone in his chest. From around his ankle he slipped out his knife and tried to wedge its blade into the cracks where light emerged. The knife was too big. He tried to ram the door with his shoulder but it held solidly. Around the bottom he felt for a heavy rock to hammer against his knife but could only find one about the size of his fist. The thought of returning to the chamber came to him, but he pushed it away. Methodically, with an almost senseless determination, he pounded the handle of his knife hoping his blade would break through and allow him to pry open the door. The effort failed. With his flippers wedged into the bottom he tried to push open the door with his shoulder. The iron obstacle remained motionless.

All hope within him vanished. The air from his tank felt thin. Reluctantly he backed himself away from the door and moved toward the cavern where at least air remained to sustain him. The criminals would come. In that case certainly they would kill him. His options had disappeared.

A faint clinking sound came to his ears. Something was knocking against the iron door, probably a fish, and thus not helpful at all. However, the pattern did not seem natural. Cautiously he swam back to the door. The noise got louder. Someone was hitting it from the other side. He took a rock and banged it three times against the door. The response came quickly matching his three knocks. He hit the door six more times and six taps answered him. He banged up to where the bolt held the door to the hinge. After a pause the taps came from that direction. The air from his tank caused him to breathe faster and more shallowly.

Miraculously the top of the door began to swing open. A hand, a woman's hand, reached through and waved at him. The other individual and himself both pulled the door and forced it open. To his utter amazement, Gabby peered back at him through her goggles as she bobbed with the current. John signaled to her that his air was out. Gabby swam over and passed her regulator to him, and together they swam towards the shore. John tried to go to the surface but Gabby pulled him back down until they had traveled about a hundred yards away from the island when she carefully directed him to the top of the water.

"Gabby, I can't believe it's you! I would have died had you not come. What made you follow me here?"

"It's a long story which I'll save for later. We don't have much time before the people who locked you up down there come back. So, let's swim to shore, get our gear off and quickly get back to our cars and go."

With several quick and powerful strokes they managed to reach the shore and then stand and lug the heavy equipment onto the beach. The whine of a small boat engine pierced the air and grew louder. Turning around they saw a small craft with three men in it racing toward them from the island. One of the men held a rifle.

Gathering their gear in their hands and dragging the tanks along the sand they rushed as fast as they could up the dune to the cars.

"Put your gear in my car, John, and I'll return it. Do you have your passport?"

"Yes. It's in my shorts with my wallet under the front seat of my car."

"Great. After you help me load all this stuff go straight to the airport and take the next flight off the island. It doesn't matter where. Just get out of here as fast as you can."

Working together they piled the equipment in the back of her rental jeep.

"What about this?" He pulled the metal box from his fanny pack. "I got it from in the cave. I also have a bunch of photos of an inside cavern in a camera."

"Give me the box. I'll give it back to you when we get to Maryland. I think you can get away from the island with the photos. That camera should be easy to hide. Bye, John. That boat is about to land on shore."

"Bye, Gabby. Thanks. I owe you. And keep that metal box refrigerated. It was stored that way."

Without another word he jumped in his car, backed it around and sped away in a cloud of dirt and dust as Gabby followed close behind. However, when they came to the main road they turned in opposite directions. John pressed the accelerator to the floor, and his car leapt ahead bouncing and jolting on the country road as the undercarriage from all the potholes. As he approached the main town, he slowed down and slipped into the slow rhythm of traffic on the island. The airport finally came into view, and he directed the car to the rental agency, left it and then went to the main terminal and changed out of the wet suit and into the only clothes with him – shorts and a polo shirt.

The next flight was boarding and would leave in thirty minutes for Puerto Rico. For a few hundred dollars John purchased a ticket and then made his way through customs and onto the flight. At long last, the plane taxied to the runway and began its takeoff. After glancing around the cabin and seeing only the tanned and happy faces of either tourists or businessmen and women, John managed to sink back in his seat, close his eyes and utter a quick thanks for what seemed to him a miraculous escape. Hopefully Gabby had managed to get back to the hotel undetected. With luck the metal box that would help unveil the mystery of Eva Bentley and her association with the Dragon cult. Clutching the camera, his only luggage, he drifted into a light sleep. Before long the plane touched down on the tarmac of the airport at San Juan in Puerto Rico. John stared out of the window at the dusty airport in the bright light.

Twenty miles off the coast of St. Martin, Le Griffon, a beautiful, white and black, hundred and forty foot yacht rose and fell gracefully in the waves. The ship had powerful, twin 2700 horsepower engines and a luxurious interior. However, carefully concealed and disguised within it were sophisticated communication systems. Even more carefully concealed was weaponry that had already sent several, pirate gunboats manned by drug runners to the bottom. In the lounge area a tall, dark man in a white polo shirt and khaki shorts sat pensively playing with a rum and coke. A beautiful woman lounged carelessly on one of the decks with a romance novel beside her untouched. Suddenly the man reached for the intercom that connected to the bridge.

"Maryland, Captain," was all he said with a slight, french accent. The ship gunned up its engines and began to turn north. The woman looked up and frowned.

Chapter XV

At the ticket counter in Puerto Rico John eyed the agent carefully.

"I'd like a one way ticket on the next available flight either to Mexico, western United States or Canada."

"Sir, would you care to narrow that down to a city and country?"

"No thanks. I want the next flight out of this airport to one of those places."

Trying to conceal her annoyance the agent punched away at her computer for a few minutes.

"There's a flight for Mexico City in two hours and in three and a half hours one for…"

"I'll take the one for Mexico City, thanks."

He paid and briskly walked away and then bought a newspaper, which he read and hid behind until his flight began boarding.

The flight delivered him safely into the Mexico City airport. Having passed an uneventful voyage from San Juan, John began to feel some measure of confidence in his choice of destination. The dragon cult would operate with its own intelligence systems and probably very sophisticated ones. It would try to figure out who and where he was and where he was going. In a matter of hours its assassins would be waiting for him in the Baltimore airport. A short stay of hiding in Mexico City might cause him to disappear from their radar and throw them into a momentary state of confusion.

As he strolled down the nearly empty corridors of the airport, fatigue beset him. The shops and restaurants were all closed or closing. His Spanish was limited but nevertheless he managed to secure a taxi. The thick fumes from poorly regulated exhausts filled the air.

"Senor, Zona Rosa por favor."

The cabbie floored the accelerator and ripped away with the smell of rubber. It didn't matter what city you were in, he thought, cabbies all drive the same way.

After a ride through a busy, dusty city, the taxi landed him in front of the lobby of a plush hotel in the Zona Rosa. Inside the lobby bustled with men and woman on business trips as well as some vacationers.

He registered under a false name and paid in cash. The clerk looked at him skeptically, eyeing the rumpled shorts and shirt and wondering about the lack of luggage. John slipped him some extra money, and the clerk smiled and handed him his room key. Great. Now he could relax. Soon he was in his room high up on one of the top floors and there jumped into bed and fell asleep before another thought of fear or doubt could disturb his mind.

The bright morning sun burst into his room, and lazily he got up and closed the curtains but not without noticing the dark clouds that were gathering in the distance. He returned to his bed and slipped beneath the covers to doze lazily for another hour before finally getting up. The sun was gone, and a gray dreariness had quickly replaced the earlier brightness. He ordered a pitcher of coffee from room service, and then collected the paper from outside his room and sat at a table to gaze distractedly at the headlines. His hand reached out to pick up the phone.

"Front desk? Yes, please, I don't want to be disturbed today. If anyone calls or asks for me tell them I won't be in until tomorrow and take a message. Gracias."

Oddly enough he felt good. The thought came to him that in this moment, in this hotel room in Mexico City, he was safe. No one anywhere in the world, who knew or wanted him for whatever reason, could touch him or reach him. The thought arose within his mind with the most delicious sense of peace and comfort. He couldn't recall feeling this way, ever, except in his childhood. He got up, opened the curtains and stared out at the massive city like someone sheltered in a cave looking out dry and safe at the raging storm beyond.

The coffee came and after sipping a cup and a half and looking through the paper without any real interest, he knew the time had come to take his next step and make plans for his return to Maryland. Hopefully Gabby would have arrived or would soon arrive so she could give him back the metal box and he could take it to the university medical center to have it analyzed. The metal box could be his rosetta stone for the operations of the dragon group.

Possibilities flickered through his mind. The technology in the cave had suggested some sort of biomedical operation. His background had allowed the easy recognition of large, cold storage systems for biological products.

He first imagined a black market trade in human organs. The demand for human organs for transplantation was very high, and a criminal group could gather quite a large profit with a constant supply from areas of the world where conflicts and small wars flared up all the time. Such a trade would require the greatest secrecy since the organs would have to transition from the illegitimate criminal world to the legitimate one of hospitals and the health care system as a whole. Any break in that cloak of secrecy would generate enormous public alarm and extensive investigations.

His second level of suspicion and one related to his first concerned the need for human embryos and eggs for couples that had fertility problems. A debate raged over the incidence of infertility. Some felt the incidence was rising. Others disagreed completely. In any case, supply of biological elements for the fertility clinics around the country was limited and very costly. Perhaps the dragon group had entered into that trade.

His musings only sharpened his interest in finding out the answers. He put down his coffee, savored one last time the peace and quiet and safety of his hotel room and made arrangements for some more appropriate clothing and his plane trip home. He was heading back to Maryland.

The next day, his arrival at the Baltimore airport surprised him by its lack of drama. He half expected men with darting, dark glances and murderous intents to be waiting for him. Nowhere did he see anyone skulking around. Only throngs of people rushing to and from gates filled the corridors. Nevertheless, he worried about what he didn't see. He proceeded in slow deliberate steps down terminal C, past the luggage checks and into the corridors leading to the other terminals. Shops and restaurants filed by. When he came to the entrance to terminal B, three young and tanned men sat on benches. They looked like some of the men from the dive shop at La Grace. In a restaurant across from them on a public phone the dive instructor with the shoulder tatoo talked angrily. Stunned, John quickly exited before he came to them and went down to the luggage pick up area and then into the parking lot to his car.

There he slowly walked around looking for any evidence of tampering. Satisfied there was none, he opened the front door. His hand froze, however, before turning the key. Suppose someone had planted a bomb somewhere? He got out of his car, opened the hood and looked thoroughly around the engine. Nothing. Then he looked under the car. Nothing. Back in the car after a deep breath, he started the engine up. Nothing. His whole being seemed to smile. Great. No violent death awaited him, at least for now. His car eased out of the lot and eventually onto the highway. His body relaxed, and his hands rested lightly on the steering wheel. The way to the medical university was well known to him.

Behind him a small silver sedan slipped inconspicuously into traffic. Three small antennae jutted out from the trunk. Never more than a few cars behind John, it followed him all the way to the university without any awareness on his part.

In the neighborhood of the medical university and hospital system, John dropped off the film at a one-hour photo place and then stopped at a public phone booth to call Gabby who was at her office.

"Hi, Gabby, this is John."

"Where are you? You dropped off the face of the earth! I thought they got you."

"No, I took a little detour, via Mexico City."

"Oh. Thank God. Where are you now?"

"In Baltimore. What happened after I left you?"

"Nothing good, I'm afraid."

"You mean they caught on to you?"

"Not at all. I've got the goods all safe and sound. No, the bad part had to do with Jack. I'm afraid we've split up. I tried to explain to him what had happened and that we should go probably home for safety reasons. Well, he didn't understand at all. In fact he became quite furious. Seems he was just humoring me all this time and didn't really care about all these investigations. This thing with you on his Caribbean vacation was the last straw. Jack's a businessman. There are only two things in life for him, business and pleasure. Everything else is a nuisance. So anyway we had a big argument. He tried to convince me to forget all this stuff with you, and I tried to point out how important it all was. I won't tell you what happened after that but it got pretty ugly. Anyway I'd pretty much say I consider him a horrible creep, and he probably thinks I'm a big bitch."

John looked down at his feet.

"Sorry about that. I have to say I feel a responsible for your problems with Jack."

"Don't worry about it. I'm glad to know what he's really made of. I shouldn't be with a man like that. He's too shallow and self-centered."

"Ok, but I still feel bad. I don't want to take you down with me. We could both end up in the gutter, you know."

There was a long pause.

"Your concern is very sweet, and I couldn't appreciate it more. Especially now. But, truthfully, now that Jack is gone I am positively relieved. The relationship didn't feel right. Getting to the bottom of the Eva Bentley murder, that does feel right."

Another long pause.

"As long as you fully understand the risks and want to stick with it, I will forever be in your debt. Thanks. Can you meet me at the Plaza near the main hospital in an hour? Would that be enough time?"

" See you then. Gotta go."

They hung up.

He walked out of the booth his steps heavy with guilt. Jack had meant a lot to her and despite her words of reassurance she would miss him. Jack misunderstood what they were doing, and certainly that was not a crime. Not many people would accept the bizarre nature of what had happened. The situation, however, was beyond his control, and reluctantly he had to stay out of it.

Less than an hour later John sat on a plush sofa in the lobby of the Plaza waiting for Gabby. People strolled in and out mostly men in suits or women dressed somewhat formally in dresses or conservative skirts. In a short while Gabby strode briskly through the door scanning the lobby and then smiled when she caught his glance. Pretty soon she was sitting beside him clutching a shopping bag in her right hand.

"Well, it's good to see you are safe and sound."

"You, too. How the hell did you find out about me in that cave?"

Gabby laughed.

"It was easy. Jack and I were sitting at a table out on the terrace while you were at the bar talking to the bartender. There was another man, someone young, in his twenties, watching you from off to the side. He was a blond, surfer type. Anyway his interest was more than casual, and I began to get uneasy. But I didn't want to talk to you directly and let everyone know that we were connected. I also didn't want my jealous boyfriend to know you were down there. Nor did I want him to feel I was more interested in you than him. The situation was setting off my alarms, however, and I kind of felt you were falling into a trap. So after you left the bar I went over there pretending to get a drink and got the bartender to tell me what he had told you."

" I gave that guy fifty bucks to keep his mouth shut."

"So much for trust and honesty. I gave him sixty bucks, and he didn't hesitate a second."

"Then what."

"Well, I had to figure out what you were up to. I couldn't exactly ask you. After you left, I waited awhile and then went up to the front desk, found out what room you were in and made up a really ridiculous story which the lady there could have cared less about. She let me know what time your wake up call was. I made mine for 15 minutes before that and then waited around to see where you were going. After you went into the scuba, shop the rest was easy."

"And you just happened to be a scuba diver."

"Well, Jack loves the islands and is an avid scuba diver. There was no way I wasn't going to learn."

"When did you know I was in trouble?"

" I never actually saw you until you came out of that tunnel. I saw a small skiff with some men in it go over to the rock face of the island. The men dove into the water for a while and then came out. I swam nearly the whole way under water to that location thinking someone might still be looking and might see me. The rest is history."

"Incredible. I have to admit I feel rather grateful to you."

She smiled.

"Oh, you'd do it for me. I have to go, John Bishop. You, get to work. I bet there's some sort of an answer for us in that box."

She handed him the box from the cave in Pig Island.

"It's been in my refrigerator."

"Good follow-through, Gabby. I'll meet you somewhere after I'm done. Sometimes I think the phones have ears so I don't think we should discuss it over the telephone."

"Don't get paranoid." She wagged a finger at him.

"Like Salvador Dali said. This is a paranoid, critical culture."

"Ok. He might have been a little bit right, and I guess you might be a little bit right, too. Frankly I've had some of the same concerns."

" Enough said. You should probably go now."

" Well, I'd love to miss all of the meetings that are waiting for me, but if I don't go, a lot of eyebrows will raise. Especially Brogan's. He's in an incredibly evil mood. Contact me when you get back. Stay out of trouble, John."

With barely another glance she got up and left. John stared after her and watched until she disappeared through the revolving doors walking. In the parking lot Gabby got into her black BMW, fired up the engine and pulled away into traffic. A brown car, noteworthy only for the number of antennas jutting out of the front and back, roared into life. The man behind the wheel, dressed in a dark tie and a dull gray sport jacket, pulled out just a few cars back from Gabby and followed her all the way to the hospital. Talking on her cellular phone, she never noticed.

John on the other hand, after watching Gabby leave, got up from the sofa and walked slowly over to the row of pay phones. His call to the nearby medical university brought the director of biomedical research on the line.

"Hello, this is Dr. John Bishop and I would like to meet with one of your genetics researchers this afternoon or as soon as possible, to take a few minutes to show him a very puzzling sample I have. I apologize for this unusual request but for reasons that I can't explain, I have an urgent need to have this sample identified. I work at a community hospital where this kind of expertise does not exist."

There was silence on the other end for a moment. Then a doctor answered, listened politely for a minute before telling him to come right over. Business-like the man hung up. Guarding the photos from the Caribbean in his pocket John clutched the metal box and with a hopeful outlook, left for the research buildings.

A short time later a man in a white laboratory coat peered through the eyepiece of a microscope rather intimidating for its technical complexity. The lab director had responded to John's request by bringing him to this lab jammed with equipment, clean and gleaming with its cold sterility. After introducing John and the researcher, the lab director had left. The man looking into the microscope was an MD/PhD and had the dry demeanor of someone used to calculating long lists of numbers and data. The scientist had pulled out two vials filled with clear liquid from the metal box. A few drops were pipetted onto his slide, and now there he sat deep in thought perhaps oblivious of his guest who waited nervously for the result.

Finally John ventured a few words.

"What do you think?"

"Yes, well, I've seen this before. I wouldn't mind running this through the DNA sequencer. Pretty damn interesting actually. Not my line of research but I know they do this over at a few labs on the West Coast."

"Do what?"

"Those vials are filled with DNA fragments. Rather rare ones. Ready to go. Ready to be spliced into some other genome."

"Are they human fragments?"

"I think so. Could be monkey or ape. I wouldn't know unless I ran some other tests."

"Could you do that for me?"

"I suppose so. Give me a month and I'll tell you what genes are there and what animal they came from, human or otherwise."

"Great. Thanks. Just give me back one of the vials and the box. The other one you can keep."

"You said you had some photos?"

John dug them out of his pocket and handed them over to the scientist who studied them carefully before giving them back to John.

"Were these taken at this university?"

"No."

"Looks like one of the West Coast medical centers," he said. "Am I right?"

"How about the Caribbean?"

The scientist looked very puzzled.

"Are you joking?"

"No. What do the pictures suggest to you?"

Instead of answering right away the scientist led him out of his lab, down the hall to an elevator and then to the basement and a locked door. He punched in the digital code of a lock, opened the door and showed John inside. There John had a sense of nearly overwhelming anxiety. He felt as if he were back in the cavern at St. Martin.

"Looks almost exactly like your photos, doesn't it?"

"Yeah. Where am I?"

"This is kind of a holding place, a genetics storage area. We keep all kinds of things down here from cell lines to organs to germ cells. You name it. The only places I know of that have places like this are medical universities and some very large corporations."

"Could an average person, if he had enough money, put something like this together?"

"Number one, all of this equipment costs lots of money. That little cold storage tank over there is over $750,000. Number two; this equipment would be of no use to anyone but scientists. Number three; all this equipment is highly controlled, regulated, tracked. So no. The average person couldn't do this."

The two men talked for a while longer and then John took his leave. Questions, endless questions. The more that were answered the more that cropped up like pesty weeds in a summer garden. A smile played at his lips. Now the tail of the dragon looked to him like the spiral of a DNA molecule. Black market genetics trade. Never in history had such a market existed. Never before had such a peril been placed at the doorstep of mankind. For millions of bucks, maybe billions kiss the integrity of the human genome away. From the labs with their awful, acrid smells, he stepped into the sun before speeding away in his car.

On the way home he stopped at a small sports bar for a quick dinner and ordered steak and french fries. The place was nearly empty except for a few burly looking men at the bar drinking beer and watching the game. The place smelled of dried-up beer, cigarettes, and popcorn, but the food was good and the atmosphere of the place took his mind off of his worries. Once he had finished and paid the bill, he went over to the payphone and dialed Gabby's number at home.

"Hello?"

"Hi, John. Did you find out anything?"

"Yes. The research people were quite helpful."

"Well?"

"I'll tell you when I see you. How about coming over to my place tonight? I'll be home in less than thirty minutes."

"I don't think you should come back here."

Silence.

"Why not?"

"Your legal situation would make that a very bad move."

"So bad I can't even go back to my own house?"

"Right. It's bad as in red hot."

John slammed his fist against the wall.

"This is the last straw. I'm going back to my job, and just let anyone try and stop me."

"Calm down. Don't fly off the handle. You can't do that."

"I know. I'd get arrested. Just letting off a little steam and venting my frustrations."

"Look. We'll have to meet somewhere else. Public enemy number one has cranked up the stakes."

"You're not referring to that pillar of the community, the honest family man?"

"Yes. His highness is using all his powers."

"Brogan has taken on the mission of destroying me."

"Us. Probably was given that mission. As we know Morgan, Morgan and Associates was hired to help him keep an eye on you. And me."

"And Stacey Simmons fell from goddess to two-faced bitch. She and Brogan would probably get along quite well."

"You'll have to explain that to me in more detail sometime. I take it you got burned. Get over it. The hospital is trying to fry you ten times over. Brogan has come out in a big way against you. He is citing some internal audit of your records that he says incriminates you in insurance fraud. He says hundreds of thousands of dollars are involved. The Feds could impound all your things including your house. Not only that there is a warrant for your arrest and there is a sheriff roaming around trying to haul you in."

"My God, my God, my God."

"Yeah, so I wouldn't think about getting back here any time soon. I'm trying to spread the word that you are still down in the Caribbean. The story seems to be holding so far. I think they even have people at the airport still waiting for you."

John's gut knotted up tightly.

"Is there anything else?"

"Not that I know of. Brogan's in a foul mood. He must have found out something about you that really soured him."

"Like what?"

"I honestly don't know, John."

"Well, do you still want to meet with me? You could be accused of aiding a fugitive."

"We're both fugitives. It's time to move fast. Do you remember the Pleasant Hill House?"

"Yeah. It's a great place. A nice bed and breakfast place in the country."

"Exactly. It's very secluded and very private. I think you ought to go there. I'll come by after I've finished what I am doing. I'm onto to something, and I need a little more time to figure it out. This'll blow your mind, John."

"You've already blown my mind."

"Get prepared for another shock then. Go to Pleasant Hill and wait for me. Whatever you do, don't go into town or show your face anywhere."

"Ok."

"Bye."

She hung up.

John stared at the phone. Aside from his family whom he wouldn't want to involve in all of this, Gabby remained his one tie to his old life and the one thread of support left to him. For some utterly stubborn reason, perhaps a very stupid reason, she was sticking to him and so far had managed to ignore the grim future that failure would bring to her as well as to him.

After paying his bill he got back in his car and slowly drove to Pleasant Hill. Despite Gabby's optimism, his situation looked hopeless. For her sake, perhaps more than his, the impulse came to flee and hide away in some bustling foreign city. Torn between two opposing needs he pressed on.

By the time he got there it was dark. He had stopped along the way to make a reservation and gave as his alias, John Knight. After a few winding roads through the country with only a house or a farm here and there amidst the forests and fields, he finally turned into the narrow drive of Pleasant Hill. Carefully tended, dark green bushes lined the narrow drive wide enough for only one car to pass through. He passed a quarter of a mile down this road into the parking lot, which held only a handful of cars. No one could be seen anywhere on the property which had one large main house built in the 18th century with a half circle of smaller guest cottages on either side. People came here for rest and relaxation and for a refuge from their busy, harried lives. Pleasant Hill certainly provided all the quiet and privacy one could hope for. For that John was grateful. The concierge was friendly and helpful and soon had him tucked away in a cottage near the main house toward one of the empty fields. The pool lay nearby but its waters had already been covered over with a tarp. White tables with colorful umbrellas still surrounded it, ready for use in the still warm, mid-autumn days.

The dinner seating had already passed, but he didn't care and picked up some cheese and crackers and a bottle of red wine from the main house to ease the tension as he sat in his cottage and waited to hear from Gabby. Most likely though she wouldn't call until morning. The building, although refurbished and modernized, remained as it was built over two hundred years ago. Over the fireplace hung numerous copper pots and pans all from a different era. Just outside on the patio laid a large jacuzzi with its warm waters always ready to spring into life at the flick of a switch.

He glanced toward the patio and impulsively stripped off his clothes, slid the glass door open, turned on the pump and then eased his tired body into the burbling water and sat staring into the darkness over the fields or into the sky where millions of stars and a half moon gave a brilliant life to the night sky. The country air was fresh and sweet. Cool breezes stirred now and then, and brought forth innumerable scents of plants and fallen leaves. Mind and body eased and a quiet sense of enjoyment and appreciation began to quell the worrisome thoughts of the day. He wondered why he had never come here before.

Out of his view a black BMW pulled into the parking lot, and an expensively dressed and attractive woman got out, walked into the main building and then without hesitation entered John's cottage.

"Hello," she called out.

John was startled but delighted to hear Gabby's voice.

"I'm in the Jacuzzi. Naked."

Without another word Gabby took off her clothes and walked out onto the patio and slipped into the water beside John who looked at her speechless.

"Oooh that feels good."

She looked over at John and then broke into giggles.

"Don't look so darned surprised, John Bishop This isn't exactly the first time." She paused for dramatic emphasis. "Don't expect anything."

"Of course not," he mumbled half-heartedly.

Gabby looked at him and then she felt herself being pulled gently toward John who held her softly around the shoulders, and together they stared wistfully out at the country night filled with stars and the gentle swaying of tall, old trees in the wind.

The, wordlessly, she turned and held his face with her hands and kissed him long and deep on the lips. Afterwards he held her for a long time not saying anything. John tried to kiss her again, but she pushed him away.

"Wait. There's something I've got to tell you. We don't have a lot of time so I have to tell you right now."

"Right now? You're going to break a wonderful mood?"

"Sorry," she said without hesitating. "It's about Ed Brogan. The man's got a lot of secrets. There is an extremely well protected file on him within the hospital computer banks. As I was looking into his relationship with the hospital board, I managed to find and read part of his file. It's in sections protected through different, very elaborate and effective security systems. Even though I am not supposed to I got access. Some of the secretaries breeched their secrecy agreements to help me partly because they liked me and respected my position and partly because they loath Ed Brogan. Of course as soon as you log into his file somebody knows. Probably I'll be found out although I took some precautions which should give us some time and maybe even enough time to do what we have to do."

"What did you find?"

"Nothing."

"All that build up for nothing?"

" Most of the information was pretty benign. Just personal info on him. Nothing to get excited about. However, there was one thing completely out of whack."

"You're usually more to the point, Gabby. Just what are you talking about?"

"Money. Lot's of it. Only there isn't much of an explanation for where it's coming from. Ed Brogan gets a base salary of $200,000 that isn't too shabby for the CEO of a community hospital our size. He gets benefits on top of that and an incentive package. For every million above 5, Brogan gets an extra $10,000. Last year the hospital made $9 million. So his bonus should have been $40,000 right? Wrong. He got $740,000. So where did the extra 700,000 come from?"

"A new clause to his contract?"

"I checked that just in case. Nothing there. Nope. There is absolutely no explanation. $40,000 came from one bank and the rest came from a foreign bank in Germany."

"Germany?"

"Yeah. I told you this gets very strange. I think some of the board members are getting huge bonuses, too. In fact with all these bonuses the hospital profit should be pretty much eaten up. But it isn't. The hospital is going ahead with all sorts of capital improvement plans."

"So Brogan is into some dirty business at the hospital."

"Must be."

"And perhaps it is tied into Eva Bentley and the charming dragon cult."

"Maybe. Brogan's been getting these huge bonuses for a couple of years now."

"Any guess as to what part of the hospital is generating this extra income for the bosses? "

"I don't know, but I have a clue. I went through departmental budgets of the entire hospital, floor by floor. Most of those budgets were ok. However, there appears to be all kinds of supplies that are going into the basement that have no reason to. IV bags and lines, lab supplies and on and on. So I got out a blueprint of the hospital and checked into the basement. There is not much there except for pharmacy, laundry, lab animals, storage rooms, security, the heating system and places for the custodians. Then, I found an older blueprint. There is a level below the basement that is not on the new blueprints. It used to be used for dining services and some other things fifteen to twenty years ago."

"And you obviously looked into how to access this level?"

"Of course. Maintenance told me there was a way down but it was restricted. You need a special pass."

"Are we stuck?"

"What do you think?"

"I think if I know you as well as I think I do we are not stuck."

"I think you know me pretty well. When I was looking into all these things I kept thinking to myself that I keep climbing further and further out onto that limb and that sooner or later that limb is going to break. On the other hand if I don't keep climbing I won't reach the fruit at the end. That must be a proverb I've heard somewhere."

John smiled.

"Well, basically, I decided to go for broke. The first thing was to actually see the entrance area. I grabbed a maintenance man who knows the building really well. I told him he had to show me the entrance to the lowermost floor. That man tried his darndest to talk me out of it. He flat out refused. I had to use my feminine wiles."

John's eyebrows rose.

"You used what?"

Gabby frowned at him.

"Your imagination is out of control." She looked at him for a moment and then smiled.

"I knew how to press the poor guy's main button which was basically a fear of authority. I told him I was second only to Ed Brogan in the administration, and as such my responsibility for the hospital equaled Brogan's and thus I had to know everything about it. If anything ever happened to Brogan, I would be in charge."

"Did he buy that?"

"Almost. He was looking pretty uncomfortable. I explained I just wanted to see it. If he didn't want to show me, I was sure his boss would. Well, he finally relented and took me to the darkest, dirtiest part of the basement where there is a very nondescript door in the wall with a digitally coded lock. You have to put an ID card into it. The digital code depends on the ID card so there are as many digital codes as ID cards."

"By the way, there is only one person the maintenance man has ever seen going through the door."

"Brogan."

"You're so smart."

"Without an ID card this information won't get us very far."

"You underestimate me, John."

"You're going to steal an ID card?"

"Not just any old ID card. I'm going to steal Brogan's. A computer friend can break the encryption on it and get the code. I've already checked it out. One of his secretaries knows exactly how to get it. Once the ID card and code are in our hands we have to move immediately because it won't take Brogan long to miss that card."

"We'd better get a lot of rest then."

"Rest isn't what I had in mind."

She kissed him again, pulling his body against hers and then slipped out of the jacuzzi.

"See you inside," she said over her shoulder.

The glass patio door slid quietly shut. John pondered what Gabby had told him and considered her plan with extreme misgivings. At this point he wanted her out of the picture because now the risks for her were escalating to dangerous levels. On the other hand she was so strong-willed she would never deviate from the commitment she had made. The best option was to execute the plan as well as possible. In the distance somewhere in the fields beyond, John noticed a small red light he hadn't seen before. Suddenly it winked out.

Eagerly and perhaps with a trace of sadness, John climbed out of the Jacuzzi, went inside and slid into the bed beside Gabby's naked body. With mounting excitement he cupped his hand around her bare shoulder and began to speak but was greeted by the regular breaths of someone who was sound asleep. Her face, peaceful and serene, lay nestled on the pillow with a single ringlet of chestnut hair draped across her cheek. He pulled the soft strand away from her eye, sighed and then dropped back into bed and quickly fell profoundly asleep.

The executioner held the axe high above his head, but his grip did not feel quite right. Anxiety rose within him. The king was looking at him closely and could see the hesitation. The executioner knew the king would be very angry if he botched the execution and didn't make a clean kill. If the condemned man died in a tortuous, agonizing way before the crowd the king would lose esteem before his people and would be considered unjust. On the other hand to make repeated false starts would be as bad. The rain had caused his grip to slip and the axe was sliding out of control above his head. His anxiety caused him to shake. Suddenly without thinking he allowed himself to drop the axe to his side. The king looked at him in astonishment and then anger. The townspeople, too, were stunned and uncertain. Never before had this happened. The soldiers, sensing the tension that was growing, held their spears and swords in a ready position. Thunder rolled, lightening flashed and the rain fell. The executioner felt the intense stares of everyone upon him and knew he had to act quickly or face a sudden execution himself by one of the king's soldiers. He seized the axe as firmly as he could and now felt it solidly within his grip. He raised it above his head summoning his greatest strength. With the immense power of his arms, he began to pull the axe down upon the man below.

When John awoke she was gone. A note was scratched hastily on a piece of paper and lay on the night table.

John,

Meet me at the hospital tomorrow night at 2am. Parking Lot J.

Gabby

Chapter XVI

The next night was darker than usual. Neither moon nor stars shone in the sky. It was one in the morning. John got into his car, started it and slowly drove down the narrow lane leading out of the bed and breakfast retreat. The beams from his headlights pierced through the mist and night air and the gravel crackled under the tires of his car. Once on the road he sped away toward the city hating to leave the quiet and security of the country. As his car raced ahead, more and more housing and shopping areas emerged until finally the city, with its tall office buildings and austere surroundings of cement and asphalt, could be seen all around.

Soon, to the right off the highway, the hospital complex came into view. A helicopter with its lights flashing could be seen slowly descending toward the landing pad on the roof of the hospital, and it no doubt was carrying some accident victim for the trauma team to handle. Most of these unfortunate patients ultimately ended up on John's service. A request for a consult usually arrived in his box on the second or third day after admission. Eva Bentley had come in on the helicopter. The thought made him wistful for his old life, which used to run along in a predetermined fashion. At this point it seemed gone forever.

He followed the exit ramp off the interstate looking carefully around and in his rearview mirror for police or state troopers that might notice his license plate. A police alert must be out for him. One police car roared by him with lights flashing and its siren blaring. When he pulled to the side of the road, the car took no notice of him and soon had disappeared into the city.

A short time later his car was easing into the vast expanse of the hospital parking lot, which lay mostly empty. During the day getting a spot was difficult, but at this time of night the only cars parked were those of the staff and those coming to the emergency room. Only a few patients had visitors who stayed overnight.

John steered his car toward parking lot J as instructed by Gabby. This one served the large, new and fairly luxurious building for the outpatient clinics. At this time of night the building would rest completely empty except for the regular security patrols. John parked his car a few rows back and turned off his lights. Another car lay a short distance away, dark and lifeless, until a door opened, and a woman got out. It was Gabby. John quickly left his car and went over to her. For a moment they embraced each other.

"Ready, John?" she said.

"I suppose."

"Anyone follow you?"

"No. How about you?"

"Nope. Let's go."

"Do you know when the security patrols go through this building?" John said following her as she quickly walked toward the entrance.

"Yeah. They just left. We've got an hour before the next one comes."

Quickly Gabby slid her ID card through the slot, and the door whisked open allowing her and John to get inside into the quiet, darkened and carpeted clinic hallways.

"Where to?" John said.

"Follow me."

They took the stairwell. The elevators had small cameras in them for central monitoring. Soon they were in the basement winding through the corridors. Only the pharmacy was open with a skeleton staff. It was open 24 hours a day, seven days a week.

Before long Gabby had led him to a part of the basement that was dirty and cluttered and full of pipes and ductwork.

"That's it," she said and pointed to a gray, metal door half hidden along a wall behind a large branching series of ducts. The only noteworthy aspect was a rectangular box with a panel of buttons and a slot for an identification card.

"You've got the card and the code?"

She nodded.

"It helps to have friends with special skills. He said this card is state of the art. It's a good thing he's such a computer nerd or he wouldn't have been able to do it."

"Well, what are you waiting for? Let's go."

Gabby swiped the card and then punched in nine numbers. She turned the knob and held the door open for John.

"Nothing to it."

"We'll see," John said skeptically.

Together they walked in to a nondescript room, dimly lit, with a door on the other side, a wooden table and three metal chairs.

"Now what," John asked.

"I don't know. I think I have to use the card again on that door over there."

Together they examined the other door, which resembled the one they had just come through in every way. Suddenly, from multiple directions, pencil thin, red beams of light fell on their bodies.

"Uh, Gabby, these are laser beams. They seem to be growing in intensity." John put his hand through one. Soon the spot on his hand began to feel warm. Several beams trained on their heads and all of the beams followed them wherever they went.

Gabby swiped the card and punched in the same numbers. The door remained locked.

"I think these lasers are trying to tell us something," John continued. "They must be on a timer. Unless you get us through that door we're going to have about fifteen or twenty holes burned clear through our bodies."

Gabby concentrated and then slid the ID card through again. She punched in nine numbers and pulled open the door. The laser beams went off. Relief.

"How did you know what to do?"

"How could I know what to do? I didn't. Not really. My friend told me he got another number out of the card. He thought it was secondary. I just guessed."

John frowned.

"I'll have to think about that later. C'mon."

The door had led them to another stairwell that went down only one flight. This time the door at the end was not locked. They opened it up and stepped into a fully lit, warehouse-sized room packed full of equipment and computers. The scope and quality of the technology dazzled them. Lab tables and equipment, desks with PC's, banks of central computer processing centers against the walls, rows of bulky items covered with white cloth stood in row upon row. A storage area like the ones at the medical center and down in St. Martin braced itself against the far wall. It was several times bigger than the ones he had seen. Throughout was the wiz and buzz of electronics and the burbling of containers filled with unidentifiable fluids. Dim yellow lights kept the area lit. The area appeared deserted.

"I don't see anyone. Let's flip on the lights," Gabby whispered.

"Don't even think about it. There's got to be a security system. Don't even move yet. See if you can tell what the system is."

They looked around but could only see cameras in the corners and in a careful grid across the ceiling.

"I think it's just the cameras. We'll have to take a chance that what we are doing is just being recorded and that there isn't anyone monitoring the system."

"Pretty fantastic, huh, John? I wonder what old Brogan is mixed up in. Everything in here must have cost millions. This is all very state of the art, right?"

"Right. Maybe even beyond that."

Gabby had already cautiously began poking around looking into this piece of equipment and then another. As she made her away around the area, all remained quiet. As far as John could tell, no alarms were tripped. No guards burst onto the scene. Whereas Gabby peered under covers and into equipment of all sorts John focused on the work on the desks and some of the papers lying on top. After fifteen minutes they met on the opposite side of the room. Both whispered.

"What is this?" she started off.

"St. Martin, the university, this place. They're all the same or rather pretty similar. This one down here actually looks like it has some bells and whistles the others don't."

"Genetic engineering?"

"A genetics products industry. According to the research scientist I saw."

"What exactly are the products?"

"I couldn't tell you yet. All these computers down here are pretty high end. I think there's a super computer in that back room."

"C'mon. Let's keep looking."

Together they strolled down the aisles. Gabby stopped at a massive rectangular object covered in a dark green nylon sheath while John walked ahead. She pulled the sheath up a bit, looked inside and then gasped.

"John, come here!"

"Hey, whisper. I'll be there in a minute."

"John, just get over here."

Irritated he ambled over. Gabby's eyes never left the object before her.

"Well, what is it?"

"Look in there. I just can't believe it. I think we ought to leave."

John peered into a smooth, clear, rectangular container. A man naked, wearing a headset of electrodes in addition to those patched abundantly around his body, laid motionless, eyes closed.

"It's you, John. It's you," she said quietly to him.

"Yes."

Numb shock filled him. The man in the rectangular, clear container lying on a metal bed with his vital signs registering on a digital display resembled him perfectly. Hair color, height, facial features, hands and undoubtedly the eyes, too, if they were open, matched his own.

"Strange to look at oneself. Bizarre."

"Incredible."

"I hate to think what the next step was for him and me."

"I'd rather not think about it."

"Neither would I."

"God, John, do you think I'm in here somewhere?"

"Let's take a look."

Before moving on John glanced at the bright red numbers on the digital display. Blood pressure 100/60. Respirations 10. Pulse 48. Oxygen saturation 98%. Temperature 95 F.

From these he guessed that the man's metabolism was artificially slowed down. The realization of what he was seeing transcended his shock and disbelief. In that glass tank laid his clone. The man resembled him perfectly, indistinguishably. There below the left knee was the same mole that John had. The hair color matched his, the shape of its lips, the build, height, the color of his skin. Of course the psychology of the individual in there could only be guessed at. There would have to be some correspondence in temperament.

What about nature and nurture?

Without his background and upbringing surely the clone would have to think in very different ways, unless of course some of that could be programmed into his mind. Those hazy moments on the boat returned to consciousness. Had some of his experience and background been downloaded, in a manner of speaking, during that time? A strange thought stopped him cold. Suppose he and Gabby awakened his clone and talked to it. What would they learn? He began to examine closely some of the technology connected to the glass case and thus to the clone. Although the actual equipment was unfamiliar to him, as he examined it, the arrangements began to make sense. There were leads to the skull that seemed to record brain activity and other leads that probably controlled brain activity. Most likely certain leads controlled traffic over the reticular activating system, those pathways that regulated the level of alertness.

"John, get over here."

Gabby's voice cut into his thoughts.

There by another glass tank she stood staring under the cover. He walked over. There was another digital panel with similar vital signs. Inside, eyes closed, lay a woman, naked, dozens of electrodes attached up and down her body but mostly onto her head. The woman was Gabby. Or rather it was her clone. John marveled at the replication of detail. Moles, tufts of hair, feet, in short every idiosyncratic feature of Gabby's body was there.

"I feel a little funny having my naked body there for everyone to see. Although I must say, my clone could use a little more time at the gym."

"Yeah, the bigger question is, when did they get your genetic material? Mine could have come when I was up in Boston. What about yours? Do you remember anything suspicious in your past? A night with strange dreams? Traumatic fears when you woke up in the morning?"

Gabby stayed silent for a moment.

"No, John. I don't remember anything like that. Except, except kind of the opposite. I am usually a light sleeper. And usually I wake up a couple of times during the night. I get a glass of water. I go to the bathroom."

"I remember."

"Well, I had a night two years ago where it was like a dark shade was pulled over me when I went to sleep. You were there, remember? I woke up eight and a half hours later as if I had been in a deep sleep, almost like some dark place I couldn't get out of. I didn't like the feeling. I almost think I had a hangover of some sort. A drug hangover. At the time I thought I felt groggy and maybe a little bit nauseous because I wasn't used to sleeping so heavily. So, I wrote it off."

"You know. I remember having weeks of nightmares after that night. Maybe that's when they took my genetic material for the clone, too. Boston must have been for something else, some other experiment or project."

John paused to think and then continued.

"The other bad thing about that is that two years ago predates this whole mess with Eva Bentley."

"Absolutely hideous. That's awful to think about. Then why were we cloned?"

"I'm not sure, but I have some suspicions. Let's try to boot up one of the computers connected to your clone. Maybe we can find something out."

John fiddled around a bit while Gabby walked around poking into things. In one of the documents, he pulled up the name of a genetics corporation. The corporation's name had appeared in national magazines for its work and success in establishing the codes of the human genome. Names of people unfamiliar to him appeared on the screen. At one point page after page of documents in Chinese script rolled past. John printed five of these pages and stuffed them in his pocket.

A gasp came from across the room.

Gabby had found two more glass tanks, and then the sound of footsteps, could be heard. It was coming from the back, a place they hadn't looked at yet. A group of people was walking rapidly toward them. John looked at Gabby and put his finger to his lips. He pointed to the exit and then motioned for her to get down to the floor. She ducked down and so did he. They crawled quickly along the floor until they came to a point where they had to leave the security and cover of the aisles to get to the exit. From the sound of the footsteps John estimated that more that three men had come into the lab area. Cautiously he peered above the level of the tables to encounter a sight that gave him the greatest surprise of the night. Four men with fierce determined expressions, guns drawn were looking about. All four were exact duplicates of one another. John estimated that Gabby and he had ten seconds to make their move.

She had poked her head out from her aisle. John held out his hand in a gesture to make her stop and then at the opportune moment motioned her forward and rushed toward the exit himself.

"Go!" he said simply as she fumbled with the ID card and code. As they let themselves into the transitional compartment the sound of the footsteps of the four security men entering the stairwell came to them. John slammed the door behind him and soon they had gone out the other door as they heard the sound of the entry door from the lab opening behind them.

"C'mon. Let's get out of here."

"Do you think they'll follow us?"

"There's no time to find out."

Sprinting and gasping now for air they rushed through the basement and then up to the clinic level.

"I don't think they're following us," John said.

"What does it matter? We've got to go."

They walked through the exit into the night air. The parking lot was empty except for their two cars.

"I want to go back. Soon. In a day or two."

"Well, you can go back without me," Gabby said definitively.

"I have to go back. It's important. I need to know more about what is going on down there. I understand if you don't want to. Probably, you shouldn't."

He gave her the pages in Chinese script.

"Get someone to translate these."

"I'll do that much, John, but then you're on your own. I've got some papers I grabbed, myself, and will get you that information, too."

The expression in her face told him she had reached her limit.

"I understand," he said. Sympathy, but also disappointment, tugged at him.

"We can't talk now. Let's go."

She stared into his face for a moment and then hugged him briefly before turning around, fighting emotions that were a mixture of guilt and fear and affection. Gabby walked quickly to her car, got in, started the engine and drove off. John stared after her both hoping that she would leave him forever and save herself and that she would never leave him and support him through to the end.

His car, dark and empty, lay waiting for him. Despondent he made his way back to the bed and breakfast deep in the Maryland countryside. Unbeknownst to him shortly after he had left, three dark vans pulled into the hospital parking lot and about twenty men piled out of them and rushed quickly into the darkened clinic building. Two hours later the men reemerged and left.

The next day John pondered the situation. He felt he had to get back into that lab to find out more information. For that Gabby had to help him. He wasn't sure if the four security guards had actually seen them. They knew someone was down in the lab due to the cameras, but for all they knew those individuals were not intruders. Their identities would be difficult to discern in the dim light. At that time of night the security detail would be obligated to investigate anyone in the lab whether they belonged there or not.

The little information that had been obtained tantalized him. This gang had pilfered a lot of information from the genetics corporation, among other sources, and clearly many applications were being used from that information. The profit potential must be enormous. He waited to hear from Gabby and worried about her emotional condition. Perhaps her fears had overwhelmed her or perhaps the strange and bizarre nature of what they had seen exceeded her ability to understand or to want to understand.

The day dragged on. He sat by his jacuzzi at a patio table with a blue cloth umbrella over it. A glass of Spanish wine sparkled in front of him, and sips from it relaxed him. His spirits began to sag until a man from a messenger service arrived with a package. Escorted by the concierge the man came around his little cabin to where John sat sullen and mellowed from the effects of the wine.

"There is the man you are looking for."

The concierge left.

"Mr. Knight?"

"Yes." The sound of his alias sounded forlorn to him.

"This package is for you. It is from a woman who was very anxious for you to have it today. I am not supposed to tell anyone I gave it to you."

Taking the brown package he stared at the man for a minute and then gave him twenty dollars. The man nodded and left. John studied the package for a moment and then sat down at the patio table with its blue umbrella and ripped away the paper. A handwritten letter lay on top of several pages of typed material. He read the letter.

Dear John,

I wish I had better news but as you may have guessed things are going rather badly for both you and me. Please tear this letter up after you have read it. Our enemies from both sides are managing to narrow down our whereabouts, as you will see from what I have to tell you. The other pages below this letter are translations of the Chinese papers you gave me. Some of it will startle you. A lot of it was beyond my comprehension and may be beyond yours as well as there is a lot of very specific scientific information on genetics.

There is discussion of multiple different programs such as clones for different purposes, organ cloning with different destinations, premium human genes that they can market and other genetic markets I don't understand. There is even mention of some very specific business contacts, names I have never heard of.

The day after our nighttime foray in the bowels of our hospital, I went back to work where the atmosphere was clearly very tense and strained. The tension came, of course, from Brogan who was in one of the worst moods I have ever seen him in. Brogan is not a man known for his good humor unless of course he is wooing potential donors to the hospital. He could be heard yelling and screaming at numerous times throughout the morning. His assistant fled from his office at one point crying and declaring that she was quitting and denouncing Brogan in every way imaginable.

Brogan called an emergency meeting. I assumed I was supposed to go. I wasn't and rather coldly was told to get lost. David was there and told me some of what the meeting was about. Brogan essentially declared all out war on you. He wants to pursue every vindictive, mean spirited action he can against you, and he wants to put you out of commission as soon as possible. All this is to happen through the Eva Bentley death. The legal proceedings will include the malpractice and negligence issues and criminal accusations, such as the manslaughter charges you have already heard about, and insurance fraud. Essentially Brogan is in cahoots with the family who is agreeing to leave the hospital out of all the legal mess if the hospital helps them in nailing you. The state medical board will be brought to bear against you as well. Your medical license is about to be history.

To top it off Brogan met with Eva Bentley's brother, that man who is passionately attached to her and who wants to see you hang in as many ways as possible. I have talked to him on the phone one or two times, and, quite honestly, the guy gives me the creeps. If he weren't rich and socially connected, maybe he'd qualify as a serial killer.

Morgan, Morgan and Associates have been very active as well and faxes from them have been coming on and off all day. I haven't been able to see much of what was in them though. They seem to be about a day behind you.

Well, that leaves me. The other day I wanted out of this and it was all too much for me to handle. I'm pulling myself together and I am ready to go back in fighting. There was a lot in that lab that I didn't tell you about. A lot of it disgusted me and a lot made me mad as hell. But the fact is, Johnny dear, I am now on the lam like you. While I was at work I was getting a lot of hostility and suspicion from Brogan. Not only that the little I saw of the faxes from the Morgan group also contained references to me and things about me, sometimes intimate things. In other words I am on the hit list. David told me straight out that Brogan no longer liked me and had plans. I've called in sick to work and am staying at a country place like yours.

What I want to say is that we have to meet. I have to apologize for losing heart and giving up at the hospital. I feel a bit ashamed about that, but I'm back on track, now. It will be hard for two fugitives to do this without risking too much, but I do know a place and it's not too far from you. There is a little run down place in the country about 4 miles from you called Charlie's. Meet me there the day after tomorrow at 12 noon.

Stay out of public until then.

Love,
Gabby

His wine glass lay empty. After filling it he took slow sips, thinking carefully, and then skimmed through the translations of the Chinese papers. Names of corporations appeared. There were references to certain processes none of which he recognized as having any counterpart within his medical education. The last page described enthusiastically the market opportunities of certain, hitherto uncloned organs such as the eye and various glands such as the thyroid and the pituitary. In the second to last paragraph one sentence set his heart thumping.

Mr. Ed Brogan has agreed through his contacts to set in motion the marketing plan for the new line of clones destined for hazardous industrial settings in Africa. If his efforts are successful this venture could prove to be one of the most profitable markets we have.

Gotcha, John thought. There it is, the smoking gun. The thought occurred to him that, with this one paper, he could stop the whole process of this criminal group at the hospital. He could go to the FBI, present this evidence and tell them what he knew. Brogan and his operation would be finished. Perhaps the whole criminal group, world wide, would come tumbling down. He teetered now between stopping with what he had and going back to the basement lab for more evidence. The thought of Brogan talking his way out of the guilt this paper indicated enraged him. He wanted evidence so damning, so overwhelming, that Brogan with all of his deceptive, slippery ways would remain firmly gripped within the federal justice system. One paper with one mention of Brogan's name was not enough. A rather daring thought occurred to him. He could take the information he had directly to Brogan. The shock of such an encounter might force Brogan into cooperating. John could exaggerate the extent of his information and evidence and thus force Brogan into some sort of plea-bargaining arrangement. If Brogan cooperated the federal authorities could do extensive damage to this criminal group and their operations.

The thought of the completion of this idea filled him with great excitement, and the numerous details that needed attention began to flood his mind. If only Gabby could help him. The rest of that day and the next were devoted to composing a proposition that would have the greatest impact. When it was complete, he rested, sat in the bubbling, heated jacuzzi, dozed on his bed, read and relaxed until evening came and the time to implement his strategy occurred.

Brogan would be most vulnerable after his dinner. Resolute, but a little apprehensive, John got into his car and once again drove down the narrow, gravel driveway to the roads. In what seemed like a short time he was pulling off the beltway and making his way into the steadily nicer neighborhoods until he reached the one where Brogan lived. Large, luxurious mansions set off from the road and set on beautifully landscaped lots of a few acres each filed past him. Brogan's success was previously attributed to shrewd investments. Shrewdness, of course, had nothing to do with his wealth.

Brogan's enormous brick and stucco house stood on Tidewater Lane. He pulled into the circular driveway and parked in front of the entrance.

Once at the door he rang the bell and waited. A woman's voice came over the intercom.

"Who is it?"

"Dr. Bishop to see Mr. Brogan. I'm from the hospital."

"I'll be right there in a minute."

A few minutes later the front door cautiously opened a few inches as a pair of brown eyes stared wide-eyed and curious. Then a latch was unfastened and the door swung wide open. A small, nondescript woman stood before him, brown-haired and friendly.

"Dr. Bishop?"

"Yes."

"Hello. I'm Mrs. Brogan. You can call me Emily. Please come in."

Mrs. Brogan took him through the foyer into a den with comfortable brown, leather sofas and a large fireplace. There were cases of guns hanging on the walls. John noted that Brogan was quite a collector not only of the older types but also of some of the sophisticated and quite destructive newer ones.

"Have a seat, Dr. Bishop. I'll get Ed. I think he was in the reading room upstairs."

The minutes ticked by. Ten minutes and then fifteen. John began to feel uncomfortable. Finally after thirty minutes Brogan strode into the room smiling. John stood up and they shook hands. The man stood over six feet tall, was slender and had neatly trimmed white hair. His eyes, cold and without sympathy, betrayed the warm smile.

"Well, Dr. Bishop, I didn't expect to see you here. You are the elusive fugitive. I guess you've heard there is quite a bit of trouble brewing for you over the death of Eva Bentley."

"That's partly why I'm here."

Brogan eyed him up and down for a minute.

"Sit down," he said taking a seat opposite John.

"I think I can help you, John." Brogan leaned forward and looked at John with deep gravity and an appearance of great compassion. The latter was clearly feigned.

"There are only a few things you need to do and then your situation and its consequences will not be as harsh they could be."

"I didn't come for your help."

Brogan pulled back, stunned.

"John, do you know how serious things are now for you? Local and state police are looking for you. You have been indicted for some serious crimes."

John stared at him for a moment.

"I know that. That's not why I am here."

"Well, I think your best option, actually you're only option is to turn yourself in. Face the music, John. The justice system looks favorably on that kind of attitude. Stop all this running around and hiding. Take what you've got coming like a man. Once you've paid your dues you can go back to a regular life. Ok, not as a doctor, but you'll find something you like. Eventually they're going to catch you. You know that, don't you?"

Brogan stared at him soberly for a moment.

"I don't think so."

For a moment the comment caught Brogan off guard but quickly he regained his usual composure.

"What are you talking about, John? C'mon. One man can't go it alone against the entire justice system. It's just too sophisticated nowadays."

"May I say something?"

Brogan eyed him suspiciously.

"Of course. Go right ahead."

"A woman on my service died. Originally I thought she was just unlucky, and that the family was taking out their grief on me, blaming me for her death. Well, I was wrong. There is guilt involved in her death."

"That's good, John. Get it off your chest. It won't kill you to admit responsibility."

"Well, the guilt belongs not to me or to one person but an organization."

Brogan's look turned cold and hard. His infamous temper was burning beneath the surface.

"This organization put a terminal device in a vein in her brain and then activated the device while she was on my service."

"John, we went over that. David told me about this silly theory. There was no device. You were unable to ever produce it."

"I am, however, able to produce the organization and yours and Eva Bentley's connection to it."

"What are you talking about, John?" Brogan spoke fiercely. He was no longer able to contain his anger. "You barge into my private home and make outrageous accusations. I wanted to be easy on you but you are forcing me to take a hard line. I am going to call the police."

"I wouldn't do that if I were you. Not unless you want to go to jail right away."

Brogan put down the telephone receiver.

"You'd better not be bluffing, John. My patience has finished."

"I've got proof positive of your involvement in a criminal organization originating out of China that, among other things, is making incredible profits off of advanced genetic engineering products. Here is a copy of a paper I have."

John handed Brogan the paper with his name on it that came from the hospital lab.

Brogan looked at it for a few seconds.

"Where did you get this?" he said sharply.

"That's irrelevant. The fact is I have it, and I would say it puts you squarely into the frying pan."

Brogan's face was turning crimson. He opened a cabinet and took out a gun. Turning pointed it at John.

"This rifle is a high powered hunting rifle. It's loaded. The safety is off. One squeeze and the bullet would tear a hole the size of a bowling ball through your chest. Or in your head for that matter. Give me one good reason I shouldn't do this."

"Gabby. She's got the originals. And the source. Kill me and in hours she'll be at the FBI's door giving them one of the most exciting leads of their lives. You'll be the first man on their list."

"What are you after, Bishop? Money?"

"Nope. Your cooperation for your life. Plea bargain with the Feds. Help them take down this cartel."

Brogan laughed loud and hard.

"Bishop. I never knew you were such a naïve idiot. Whatever possessed you to come here in the first place? My life. Cooperate with the Feds. Good, God! I could do that and before I got two words out of my mouth I'd be dead. The one thing that surprises me is how long you've managed to live. You're such a goddamn idiot. I would have believed you more if you had asked for money. Now get out. I would like to blow you apart. But I wouldn't want to upset my wife with all of your blood everywhere."

He put the gun back in its case.

"Emily! Come here! Dr. Bishop is leaving now. Please show him to the door."

"You've always known about Bentley's death, haven't you?'

Brogan paused for a moment.

"Of course, damn it! Eva Bentley was a beautiful, talented girl but she was headstrong and so she got into trouble. We had you picked to be the fall guy. You were too nice and naïve."

John stared at him with resentment burning in his chest.

"Well, it looks like you miscalculated."

"A little. But not much. It'll all be the same in the end. I work for a very efficient and competent organization. Loose ends do not appeal to them."

Quiet and subdued Brogan's wife came into the room. She glanced quickly at John and then looked at the floor. She apparently had heard the sounds of the argument from the next room. She showed him through the front door and never looked at or spoke to him again.

In the night air John felt the adrenalin pumping through his veins. The sounds of the night came to him in amazing clarity. A door slammed shut. Someone played basketball at a house nearby. Some kids walking down the street talked and laughed loudly. He got into his car and drove quickly out of the driveway. He knew he was racing against whatever Brogan planned to do versus whatever he and Gabby could do. In forty-eight hours one of them would win. The struggle would be over.

His car slipped quietly through the deserted streets. He gazed ahead, to the sides and in his rearview mirror looking for cars that might be following and people on the street who might have guns. The streets were absolutely empty. The houses were lit up through the trees, and he glimpsed here and there families sitting down at dinner, talking on the phone or reading. For a moment, a brief moment, the banality of his surroundings inspired him with feelings of peace and serenity. His being yearned for such normalcy. Brogan be damned, he thought. The roar of a motorcycle cut through these feelings like a knife. The motorcycle pulled up closely behind John with its headlights flooding into his car so he couldn't see the driver. Seconds later another motorcycle joined the first one. John sped up and so did the other two. He slowed down and they began to come up beside him forcing him to pick up speed again. The game of cat and mouse had started.

Up ahead a stoplight glowed green but then suddenly turned yellow and red. John drove straight through it and the motorcycles followed. Behind them a large truck drove up. It was large enough to hold a car. Another stoplight loomed straight ahead but this time it stood over a busy road where cars rushed steadily back and forth. John would have to stop at that light. It was turning red. As his car came to halt one of the motorcycles pulled lazily alongside his door. The driver sat only a few feet away but carefully concealed his identity under a helmet with a dark face guard. Jacket and pants in black leather hugged his muscular body. The man was reaching under his coat and began pulling out an automatic weapon made of a dull black metal.

For a moment they stared at one another. The man in black staring out from the shiny black plastic visor looked like one of the ancient furies stepping straight from the gates of hell. The gun that could unload dozens of high velocity bullets in seconds began to swing into position. With a speed and force that surprised both the man and himself John flung open his car door and kicked it into the motorcycle knocking the bike and the man down. The gun went skidding over the asphalt. To the other side the gunman had started to pull out his automatic. He had moved forward to avoid having the passenger side door knocked into him. John pulled the steering wheel hard to the right and then jammed on the accelerator and his car caught the front wheel of the motorcycle sending it and the driver spinning into the ground. Without a second thought John sped through the red light into the traffic cutting off a car that blared its horn for one eternal moment. John estimated he had less than a minute to shake the two men. A series of maneuvers brought him through some side streets and then onto another avenue lined with large luxurious homes. The street was dark and quiet.

He rolled down his window. The roar of motorcycles was coming closer. High above him was the sound of a helicopter descending. He turned off the headlights of his car and cruised down the darkened street for several hundred yards. To his left was a large, English Tudor mansion with a yard heavily landscaped with trees and bushes and a hedge. He turned his car into its driveway, drove toward the back, under and behind some trees, as far out of sight as possible and turned off the engine. Some of the windows shone brightly with lights and revealed a family relaxing. Teenagers gathered around a TV. A mother and father sat reading in a living room. As quietly as possible John got out of the car and crawled to the front hedge. The motorcycles were coming down the street. John dropped to his belly and crawled up to the hedge under a holly tree to peer through onto the street. No one would be able to see him from the street or from above. Or so he hoped.

The two motorcycles came slowly abreast of one another. The men gunned the engines, which roared into life and then subsided. One man looked down the left while the other scoured the right side. Their guns lay ready across the handlebars. John waited anxiously for them to pass the house. They did so without hesitation. At the end of the road they stopped. One of the men pulled out a walkie-talkie, talked for a few minutes and then put it away. The two men turned their motorcycles around and waited. Minutes later the helicopter came down to the street hardly a hundred feet above the ground, violating half a dozen FAA rules. The helicopter switched on a searchlight and slowly made its way down one side of the street and then the other. Its searchlight swept all through the different lawns and occasionally into darkened windows. Angry people stuck their heads out of windows and glared up at the helicopter yelling into the deafening roar of its blades. Trees and bushes swayed beneath the downdraft. These same people must be calling the police. For a few brief seconds the searchlight swept over John and a few shafts of light managed to penetrate the layers of leaves and branches and spot his shirt with flickering white light. By some grace, the helicopter did not stop. After a few minutes the helicopter and motorcycles were gone. John climbed into his car and drove away. In his rearview mirror he could see two police cruisers just turning onto the street with their overhead lights flashing as he himself sped away down a side street.

Slightly less than an hour later he steered his car down the narrow gravel road to the bed and breakfast. The now familiar bushes lay on either side of him. He rolled down his windows. The soft, nighttime country air wafted into his car with its cool, freshness and brought with it the sounds of scattered birds, insects and dead branches falling to the dead leaves below. For one sacred second peace and safety filled his consciousness.

The man waited for the moment when the blade of the axe would come slicing through his neck. He couldn't understand why his death hadn't come swiftly like that of the others. He was beginning to shiver within the dirty and wet robe that covered him, and his discomfort was mounting. There was no fear, just a mind aching with confusion. His life had been devoted to the healing of others, especially the poor, and somehow this had brought upon him the worst punishment of the land. Abruptly an immense flash occurred. The air smelled of electricity and burning flesh and then the thunk of a fall and the clanging of metal against stone came to him. A boot was pressing roughly into his leg. For a moment afterwards, only the sound of the rain falling lightly sounded to him beneath his hood. The shouts of men tore through the air, and someone ripped the hood off of his face. There behind him, the executioner laid dead from a strike of lightening. His hood had rolled half off of his face and the man recognized the executioner. He had helped his wife with a difficult childbirth once and had saved her life. The man turned to the king who looked puzzled and almost desperate. The townspeople were looking to the monarch to act. The king knew that the lightning was seen as an act of God, and that the townspeople recognized only one authority higher than his own. To kill this prisoner now, someone he dearly wanted dead, would spread discontent within his kingdom. As harsh as his rule and laws were, such discontent could easily gather power and become the seed for revolt. The soldiers stood waiting for his orders.

Chapter XVII

The following morning was filled with urgency. He knew Brogan and his organization were operating at a red alert status, scouring the region for him and for Gabby. As the time slipped away the chances of them failing a second time were almost nonexistent. Every few moments he would stop and listen and then peer cautiously into the driveway. Nothing but the sunny peacefulness of nature greeted him. The orange, red and yellow autumn leaves looked beautiful. Guests strolled leisurely around. Cars came and went. Nothing suspicious occurred.

He drove down the gravel driveway and directed his car quickly to the diner. In the parking lot of the diner were a few battered pickup trucks and an old sedan but nowhere did John see Gabby's car. Cautiously he parked and walked inside. There was Gabby sitting at a booth. Although a faint smile of greeting played at her lips, her eyes were lined with tension, worry and fatigue. John fretted inwardly about her determination and morale. He sat down across from her. The place smelled of cigarette smoke and odors from frying foods.

"Hi. Where did you park?"

"I took an extra precaution and parked down a side street near here."

"Good idea. I should have done that myself."

"Anything wrong?"

"A lot. Let's order first."

Neither of them was very hungry but nevertheless they gave the waitress their order for French fries, cokes and sandwiches.

"Okay. Tell me what's up. I take it we're not talking good news," Gabby said warily.

"No we're not. I think I made a big mistake last night."

Gabby frowned.

"What did you do?"

"I went to Brogan's house."

"What?" Gabby gasped and looked away. "John, how could you do that?" She had lowered her voice in an attempt to control her instant anger.

"I tried to force him to turn himself in using the papers we have. I didn't count on the fact that his fear of this group is bigger than his fear of the authorities. Also, I didn't realize that he considers them more powerful than the authorities."

"You took too big a risk. You threw away all options."

"No. We've got one last chance. A good one. Don't panic. Let me tell you what happened before I go into that."

For the next fifteen minutes John recounted the course of events of the night before while Gabby sat quietly, completely incredulous and caught between amazement, concern and anger.

"I've gotta say, John, you're story makes me think we're finished. Either Brogan and his buddies get us and probably kill us and dump us in the river somewhere or else the police catch us and lock us up for the rest of our lives on God knows what series of charges. Take your pick. I say we turn ourselves in. With the help of some good lawyers maybe in ten years and with good behavior, we can go back to having a somewhat normal life. Besides the papers I took tell me they are getting awfully close to catching up with both of us."

"What do you mean?"

"Someone in their group has been hacking into the computer lists of guests in the hotels and inns around the city."

"So? I signed in under an alias and paid cash. You know that."

"I also know that they figured that and are looking at people who paid cash for their rooms. Paying cash is pretty unusual these days. Especially at your place."

"Get to the punch line. What did you find?"

"There are less than ten people who paid cash for rooms around here. John Knight at Pleasant Hill is close to the top of that list. The sooner you check out, the better off you'll be."

"They must be looking for you, too."

She nodded her head.

"See what I mean, John? We've got to turn ourselves in."

"There's another option."

"Yeah? Well, right now I'm feeling pretty damn skeptical. Most of our activities have driven us deeper and deeper into trouble. But go ahead. What is it?"

"We go back into the basement lab at the hospital and get more evidence. From what I can figure, out these guys are on the verge of taking over the hospital completely. Once they do that, no one's going to catch them. The administration will be completely under their control either with the clone replacements or with stooges like Brogan. So, if we give up the hospital is gone."

"And when do we do this foolhardy thing?"

"Tonight."

"What makes you think they won't be waiting for us? Those guards, those four monsters, were coming after us the last time we left that place. Don't you think they would have made a nice, interesting report to their bosses?"

"I don't know that they saw us. I think they came out only because some kind of alarm went off. I think we made a clean escape. Anyway we have to take that chance. Going to Brogan's made me realize just how much evidence we need to put his group and him out of commission. Only that basement lab can give us that kind of evidence."

Gabby was silent for a long time and stared fixedly off into the distance. Finally she answered.

"Ok, John. Maybe you're right. But I've got a bad feeling. I think Brogan will be waiting for us.'

John smiled.

"If you can think of another alternative, we can talk about it. Otherwise, I'll see you there tonight. One in the morning should do it."

"Well, I've got something to tell you, too. While you were gawking at your clone in that lab I went around peaking into other tanks and even went back to another room."

"Yeah, I know. I remember wondering what had happened to you."

"It's a good thing I did. There were a lot of tanks, some like the one your clone was in and some that were different. There were all kinds of people in those tanks all of whom I didn't recognize except for one."

"And who was that?"

"Brogan."

"What?"

"That's right. I think they are planning on getting rid of him. Maybe with this Eva Bentley thing they think he's screwed up badly."

"I wish I had known that before I saw him."

"Sorry. I obviously didn't know you were going to do that. The other storage tanks had organs in them. Containers were clearly labeled. Kidneys, livers, hearts and others."

"Illegal trade in organs. That alone would put you behind bars for a long time."

"And I can't wait to see that happen. What I want to know is where did those organs come from."

"You mean like from clones? Or are the organs themselves cloned individually?"

"Right. Perhaps they take these organs from people they have killed. Also, designer genes. That metal box from the Caribbean must have contained designer genes. Better looks, better brains, better athletic powers. Every gene, every chromosome has a price tag. Every clone a bigger price tag."

"Probably all of the above are part of their operations and more."

The food came and silently they munched on french fries and sandwiches.

"Ok, John, so we go home, keep a low profile and then go back to the hospital at one."

"That's right. You got Brogan's pass copied, didn't you?"

She nodded.

"OK, then. See you tonight. Let me remind you to watch out for those guys on the motorcycles. At this point they are hunting you as well as me. And don't be late. If you're more than 10 minutes late I'm going to have to come looking for you."

Gabby smiled.

"Yeah, ok, so I tend to be late. I'll be there on time."

They got into their cars and left.

At precisely one o'clock that night John sat in his car in the parking lot of the hospital near the outpatient clinics waiting for Gabby to arrive. His car was the only one in this particular lot and he felt very conspicuous sitting there in the dark. Five minutes later he began to drum his fingers in irritation. Gabby had to be late. It was just like her. The more important the occasion the more likely she was to be late. At ten minutes after one, worry replaced irritation. The only movement he saw was an ambulance heading in the opposite direction for the ER.

Reluctantly he slipped his key in the ignition and started up the engine. As he slipped the transmission into gear he saw a pair of headlights winding their way toward him. The car parked a short distance away, and its lights went out. Gabby got out of the car and walked quickly for the darkened side of the building. John followed.

"Hey, where the hell were you?"

"I had to duck those guys on the motorcycles. I saw them cruising around the neighborhood I'm staying in. I don't think they saw me."

"Let's hope so. After we finish here tonight you can come back with me. You'll be safer where I am. Now let's go to the basement. We've got a lot of work to do."

Together they hurriedly slipped inside the building and quickly reached the bottom floor where the entrance lay. Only a few late night workers were seen, and those were too busy to notice them. Having gone through the routine once before, Gabby easily guided them through the doors and locks and in minutes they were descending the steps that led to the basement lab.

Once inside the lab they stood silently for a moment. It lay in a dim light with the sound of electronic equipment buzzing and crackling and small colored lights blinking on and off here and there like mechanical fireflies. Other than themselves, nobody was around, nobody up and moving that is. They were surrounded by beings ready to come awake and emerge into some sort of twilight existence.

"OK," John said breaking the reverie. "Let's go. We need evidence that can be used against Brogan and his organization. We should go in different areas to make the best use of our time."

Without another word they dispersed through the lab. John went straight for the glass case holding a body seemingly identical to his own. Would the body express a personality like his? Was it a clue to his own self, his own identity? His eagerness made him oblivious to his surroundings. He removed the covering and there his clone lay virtually without change. One important change had occurred, though. The vital signs were basically normal. Respirations were now 16. Pulse was 78. Blood pressure was 124/72 and the temperature was 98.2 F. John surmised that the clone was in the process of being activated. Now, instead of being in a deep coma, it was probably held in a light stage of sedation.

John began toying with the PC. Various readouts of data were displayed. One in particular worried him. It indicated a heart defect, not immediately lethal but one that could shorten a lifespan. Some of the readings he understood and some were completely foreign to him. He wanted to activate, to awaken his clone. Gabby, however, was calling to him from a back room. He quickly walked over to her.

"Well, what?" he whispered impatiently.

"Look," she said pointing. Her expression was forlorn.

She was pointing into another case. The light inside, however, was dim and he found it difficult to tell what was inside. The red digital readout of vital signs showed, except for some mild hypertension, a normal physiologic state. From his pocket he took out a small flashlight connected to his keychain and flashed it into the case. To his shock he saw the body of David, the hospital risk manager. Multicolored tubes streamed from out of his abdomen.

"Do you think it's his clone or David?"

"I don't know. Let me look around a little."

In a moment he had found the PC relegated to his friend David and soon various data were coming up on the screen.

"There's a list of illnesses connected with this body. I recognize most of these as belonging to David. I think this is the real David."

"Are you sure?"

John studied the computer for a few minutes.

"No question about it. David had a small heart attack once. An anterior MI. It's all here."

"Can you wake him up? He was, I mean is, you know, our friend."

"I know. He did try to help me. It doesn't matter whether he was our friend or not. I wouldn't want this to happen to anybody."

"So, you'll wake him up?"

They both stared at the body of their friend lying in the glass case, motionless except for the barely perceivable motion of his chest. Eight breaths per minute. Very slow. He was in some kind of heavily sedated state.

"Can't be done."

"What?"

"Can't be done."

"Why not?"

"He is missing a good portion of his liver. In his current rate of metabolism that doesn't seem to affect him. However, if I were to wake him up, his metabolic rate would rise and the liver function just wouldn't be there. I think he would die."

"Well, what are we going to do, John? We just can't leave him there like that."

"We'll just have to move our plan ahead. When we get out of here tonight we'll have to make sure the FBI or somebody gets in here and takes control of this lab and gets David the right kind of help."

"So, if that is David, does that mean I have been talking to his clone the past few weeks?"

John scanned some more of the files.

"Yup. David has been down here since the whole thing with Eva started."

Gabby was silent for a moment.

"In a lot of ways David was kind of irritating. But you know I always thought of him as a friend. He helped my career."

"I just thought of something. Not only have you been dealing with David's clone but I have also. When I told David about the microchip device in Eva's brain, I unknowingly gave the information to the wrong David. That's why someone stole the device from my desk drawer, and someone decided to blow up Flexner's lab. Sickeningly effective, aren't they?"

"Yes, they are. And now look at poor David."

"There is nothing we can do right now. My plan is to come back and get him once I understand more. Come on. Let's get back to my alter ego. I'm going to wake him up."

"What!"

"I figured out how to do it."

"John, we've got to get out of here. Someone could find us at any moment and kill us."

"It won't take long."

Completely exasperated, Gabby sighed and followed the real John to where the naked John lay in the glass case, eyes closed, peaceful.

"I think I'm going to stay over here," Gabby said and stood off behind some equipment. "Who knows what a clone might do. Maybe it is violent."

John started to send commands into the computer. The vital signs started to change. The pulse rate quickened and the blood pressure rose a few points.

"He's pretty close to being awake as we speak. I just have to cut off the sedatives flowing through his IV and do some other things and voila! I come face to face with my mirror image. The opportunity is too much to miss."

"To hell with your curiosity! When it's time to leave, it is time to leave. I've got photos, papers and some of the smaller bits of technology to take with us. Grab your evidence and let's go!"

"Don't get nervous, Gabby. I want to do this one thing and then we should make sure we've seen everything and make sure that what we have is enough to put a real dent into this group, maybe even finish it off. Brogan is going down. Look!"

They both stared into the glass case. The right arm of the clone had twitched. Then abruptly the right hand opened and closed.

"The only thing going into his veins now is a dextrose and saline solution. The sedatives were short acting. He should wake up any minute."

Almost as if expecting an explosion Gabby stepped back several feet. She looked scared and very unhappy. The clone's eyelids were still shut but his eyes underneath were moving rapidly. His right hand reached up and scratched his forehead, and then both hands rubbed his eyes, which opened abruptly. He stared above and his face twisted in confusion and it seemed to John, some pain as well. The heart rate had climbed to 102 and the pressure had gone up a bit. Wide-eyed, somewhat confused he looked all around. Hands reached up to feel the wires attached to him. The thought occurred to John that the clone was about to panic and that such a panic could put all three of them in a lot of jeopardy. John walked over to the glass case, opened the top and stared and smiled at the clone.

"Hello," he said. "How do you feel?"

A face, his own face, looked back at him in utter confusion. The response came in a whisper.

"Where am I? Did I get sick?"

Dumbstruck John just stared at him for a moment. The voice was nearly identical to his own.

"You're in the hospital."

This answer confused the clone even more.

"How could that be? I remember being in my house and now all of a sudden I am here. Did I get sick?"

"Not exactly. Let's leave that for a moment. Can you tell me who you are?"

"Why I'm, I'm..." For a moment the clone seemed at a loss. Then his face brightened.

"I'm John Bishop. Dr. John Bishop."

John nodded.

"Where do you live Dr. Bishop?"

"Uh, 85 Shadyview Drive."

Amazing, John thought. Correct.

"Can you tell me who you're younger sister is?"

"Sure. Angelica. She lives in Los Angeles. She's an actress."

The clone certainly had some basic facts of his life down pretty well. He would try something harder.

"When you were young, age 8, you had a bicycle. What color was it?"

The clone thought long and hard.

"Red. It was red."

Aha! John was excited. His bicycle at that age was blue. He'd never had a red bike. John got up close and looked at the clone straight in his face, about a foot away.

"Do you know who I am?"

A short pause ensued.

"No. I don't know you. Do you work at the hospital? Are you another doctor?"

"Yes, I am."

The clone sat up and stared over the edge of the case into the room.

"This really is a strange place. Why are there no nurses?"

At this point he spotted Gabby. His face melted into a warm smile.

"I should have known you would be here," he said to her as Gabby recoiled a bit. "Can you come over here where I can see you better."

Gabby looked at John who nodded. She came up to the case. The clone reached out for her hand and reluctantly she gave it to him. Tenderly he raised it to his lips and ever so gently kissed it.

"I love you darling," he whispered to her. "Why am I here? I hope this doesn't delay our wedding." Gabby pulled her hand away and walked rapidly back to the shadows. She looked at John and pulled her hand across her throat angrily.

"Stop this!" she whispered fiercely.

However, John's curiosity had mounted uncontrollably.

"Is Gabby your fiancee?" he said.

"Yes. We're getting married next week. I've been under a lot of stress at the hospital, but all of that has been resolved now. I've been in love with her since the day I met her."

John began to feel uncomfortable. Until this moment he had never realized how intense his original feelings for Gabby had been. The times of conflict had somehow covered up this fact, but now the clone was baring such emotions out in the open, something he had never done to Gabby in the past. Gabby was pacing, and now as if the last straw had been broken, she strode forcefully toward the exit.

"Bye, John," she said. "I hope you have fun with your clone."

"Wait. Ok. It's over. I'll put him back to sleep."

She stopped and turned to look at him.

"Do it. Now," she ordered.

"Is something the matter," the clone asked concerned. "I'm sorry I've upset you both. Gabby, did I tell our secret? Sorry, dear. We'll just have to ask this man to keep it under his hat until we make the announcement."

"And when is that?" John couldn't help but ask.

"At the monthly medical staff meeting."

John and Gabby looked at one another.

"John, right now," Gabby said sternly.

After returning to the computer, John had programed the flow of sedatives back through the IV and the clone dutifully lay down and closed his eyes. John closed the lid on the glass case.

"He was a nice guy. I like my clone. I didn't know you two were so familiar."

"You're not funny."

"Sorry. Do you want to waken yours?"

"No. One of us is all I can stand for the night. The idea of talking to my clone doesn't quite appeal to me as much as it does to you."

"You ought to try it. You'll never again be able to stare into the face of someone who has the exact same DNA as you."

"Exactly right, Dr. Bishop!" The voice boomed through the lab. It was Brogan's coming over some kind of PA system. John and Gabby looked at one another and immediately began to run for the exit.

"Try if you like, but running is useless. I've been watching you the entire time you were here."

The four guards, all precisely alike, suddenly appeared and began to close in on them. One of them blocked the exit and pointed an automatic pistol at them. The other three quickly grabbed John and Gabby. Their strength and agility were unnerving. Very quickly the guards had duck taped their wrists behind their back.

"I guess you were right, Gabby," John said looking down at his feet. "I'm sorry I brought you here."

Before Gabby could respond Brogan burst into the room with an entourage of several men and woman and came to a stop in front of them. He was smiling with cold hatred and pleasure.

"At last our little sporting match is over. It had to end this way. As I tried to tell you, Dr. Bishop, the power of this organization is unlimited. You have no idea. I rather like the street name for it, you know, the Dragon's Tail. Its power did come from China originally, but China is no more responsible for it than any other country. Now it is like a global, multinational company. It spans all borders. It's reputation for ruthlessness is quite deserved. The fate of you two will be a little more conventional than that of your friend David. The sale of some genetic products milked from your bodies will make us quite a pretty penny. He, on the other hand, is quite graciously allowing us to perfect techniques in trans-species genetic combinations. Bugs, plants, mammals. They all can provide some unique advantages when their genes are combined."

"By the way, Dr. Bishop, you were quite correct in not waking up your friend. It would have killed him. I regret to inform you that David can never be woken up. But you are wrong to assume that any organs are produced here. This lab is a cloning station, and that is all. Some cloned organs are transhipped from other production stations, but none are produced here. And pretty soon both of you will be lying in a nice glass case like him. That is until we have made maximum use of your bodies and genetic material in our various production lines. Then, in a quite natural fashion your bodies, worn out, will die."

"But the world outside will never be the wiser. David's clone will function like a mindless idiot doing whatever I say. Your clone and Gabby's will manage their little worlds and live in relative poverty as most of the money they earn goes to paying off the huge settlement to Eva Bentley's family for the malpractice suit you will have lost. For your criminal convictions you will be placed, through the kindness of a judge paid off by our organization, on probation for an indefinite term. See how nicely all of the details are tied together? Don't you like such perfect endings?"

He laughed slightly and then motioned to the guards who started to lead the two away.

"You're fucking up our biological heritage!" John yelled after him.

Red-faced Brogan turned around and came within inches of John and jabbed his fingers into his chest.

"You're an asshole, Bishop. A sentimental, bleeding-heart asshole. The world has changed. The human body isn't some sacred vessel we can look upon with some sloppy, whimpy sense of identity. Genetics has changed all that. The body is like the goddamn car. We can crank it out one after the other on an assembly line, and just like car parts we can crank out the organs. Genetics technology did that."

He jabbed at each organ in turn.

"Your lungs, your heart, your liver. All of you. Price tags everywhere. Some of us get rich off of this. And that's what it's all about. And some crappy rehab doctor is not going to get in the way. Get it? One clone, just one, earns ten million dollars. This lab alone makes over a billion every year."

Abruptly one of the guards dropped to the floor with a small bleeding hole through its forehead. A minute or two later the other guards dropped down as well. Blood pooled around them. Men began to shout. Brogan's expression turned angry and then frightened. His face was white.

Nearly thirty men in black kevlar and black shirts and pants and helmets rushed in with automatic weapons drawn. They quickly surrounded the small, frightened group and pushed their weapons underneath the chins of Brogan and John and Gabby and the others. Nobody dared move or speak. A man in a black suit with a dolphin tie came in. The man sauntered up to the group as the men in black swat suits tensely waited. Without a word the man in the suit motioned to Brogan and his entourage who were instantly escorted away.

"Dr. Bishop, Miss Stavros, follow me," he said and walked away. John and Gabby looked at each other and then followed the man who walked down an unfamiliar hall and then through various doors and stairs until they found themselves walking out onto the asphalt of the outside parking lot. Dozens of cars and trucks were scattered around. Helicopters stood here and there as their blades still whirred with life. The man led them into the back of a van without any windows. Inside there was equipment and seats bolted to the floor.

"Sit down," the man said.

Obediently John and Gabby sat down.

The man sat back in a chair. He smiled.

"Thank you," he said.

John and Gabby looked at him puzzled.

"Thank you, Dr. Bishop. And Miss Stavros."

"I don't understand," John managed to whisper.

"It's simple." The man smiled. He was clearly enjoying the superiority of his position. "Quite simple. Don't you get it?"

"No I'm afraid I don't."

"We've followed you, Dr. Bishop. From the moment Eva Bentley was your patient we followed you. Before she was your patient we followed her. You never knew what you were getting into. We did. I'm sorry. You almost didn't make it. Fortunately for us you are a resourceful and determined man. If you weren't, we of course would be out of luck."

"You knew about this all along?" John asked incredulously and with some disgust.

"Well, yes. The Dragon's Tail. We're at loggerheads with them. They are getting quite powerful. In fact their power is getting to the point where they could overwhelm us. But thanks to you, we've dealt them a terrible blow."

"Are they destroyed?" Gabby whispered.

"I'd like to say so. But no. They are not destroyed. They live. They are extremely tenacious. We've won a battle. A great battle. Your lives are spared but unfortunately the war persists."

"And what is the war?" demanded John.

"No less than the soul of mankind."

John looked at him skeptically.

"I mean that, Dr. Bishop. Only necessary secrecy prevents me from telling you what I mean. Chemical warfare. Biological warfare. Nuclear weapons. All of these exist, but in comparison to what the Dragon's Tail represents, they are all children's toys. Genetics for instance. That poses a much greater threat. Genes, chromosomes, DNA. Look into your DNA and you see the face of God. Evil men playing with the tools of God."

"So. Who are you?" Gabby demanded.

"Not for you to know. Not at all for you to know. Normally you would never meet me. Perhaps, also, there would be no effort on our parts to intervene for the sake of your lives. But again sanity prevails. Sanity in an insanity of destruction. Where great destructive weapons exist there is always insanity. Don't you agree?"

John and Gabby nodded their assent.

"Well. Well. We've decided to give you a helping hand to live. I like you both. If I didn't well let's not talk about that."

He leaned forward for emphasis.

"I like you and trust you. Trust is very important in my relationship with each of you. Do you understand what I am saying? Thousands of years ago an eastern philosopher said, "Whereof we can not speak, thereof we must be silent." My organization wants just that. Silence. Do I make myself clear?"

"Yes," John managed to whisper.

"Perfectly," Gabby echoed.

"Good. We have an understanding. There is more than life and death in all of this you know. There are greater issues. You've done your part. Now, like good actors you must leave the scene. But don't be fooled. Good actors are in demand. Your casting call may come again, and if it does, once again, you won't know it until the scene, the act has finished."

John and Gabby got up to leave.

"If you break your promise we will know. We know your every move, almost your every thought. When you leave here there will be a checkpoint. The guard will be notified that you are coming. He will ask for a password. Tell him, 'storybook'. Now leave."

The back of the van opened up. Hesitantly John and Gabby got up and filed out of the van. Outside the tumult continued. The helicopters were taking off. Some of the large trucks were roaring into life and leaving. Men in black swat suits and machine guns dotted the parking lot. Other trucks were still being loaded with items covered in cloth. John and Gabby quickly went to their cars.

"Well, I'm going home finally," John said somewhat disbelievingly.

"I don't think the danger is over yet."

"It'll never be over, but I am feeling a little more secure."

"Are you going back to work?"

"Eventually. After I talk to my lawyers. We'd better go. I'll call you tomorrow."

Gabby's hand reached up to his shoulder.

"Do you want to come to my place?"

"Thanks, but I need some time to sift through all of this."

She nodded understandingly and gently kissed him.

Without another word they got in their cars and sped away. Just before the checkpoint John glanced over his shoulder and looked back. Only one truck remained and it was already pulling out. My God, they work fast, he thought. There was no doubt in his mind that not a single item of the lab remained in the hospital basement. All of it within an hour or two had been carted out to be driven to some secret, federal destination where the information and materials would be analyzed in every manner possible. Surely the information obtained would lead to more victories against the criminals. But like the man with the dolphin tie said, the victories were only over battles and not the war. He wondered what would happen to his clone and to David for that matter.

The king rose to his feet. All of the town and all of the soldiers turned to him. He motioned to his guards to bring the prisoner to him, and soon the man came before the king and kneeled. The king began a great speech. God, he said, has shown us his mercy today in giving us a sign to spare this man's life and to give him a pardon for the sins he has committed against his king. From this point on the man shall go forth in freedom and he is spared his punishment and his sentence shall be erased from the courts of law. Immediately there was the murmur of ascent and the approving nod and smiles of the people. The lightening strike had stirred great fear among them, and had the king chose not to spare the man surely God's wrath would mark the land and great suffering would ensue. War, plague, drought, any number of calamities might burden their lives, already quite arduous. The king felt the approval of his people. The man's shackles were removed and he walked away from the town and away from the crowds and headed to the country. The king adjourned the executions and the rest of the prisoners were led back to the prison. Once the procession had left the town, the king summoned four of his soldiers and told them to go and find the man, kill him and dispose of the body where no one might find it.

Chapter XVIII

The following day John woke up with a start. He looked out his window. There was a car parked in front of his house with a man inside reading a newspaper. It was the same man who had followed him home last night. He slumped back in bed. 9:30 in the morning. Was he safe?

Katie would appear any moment to deliver his two dogs. He could see her coming down the street with Humphrey and Groucho on leashes pulling her along, almost whisking her off her feet in their eagerness. Before they could get to the front door he had opened it and ran outside into the sunlight to greet them. The two dogs jumped all over him, barking and trying to lick him while he petted them furiously with immense affection.

"Well, they sure missed you, Dr. Bishop."

"I think I missed them more. I want to thank you, one my friend, for taking care of them."

He bent over and kissed her on the forehead.

"I asked my mom if I could keep them forever, and she said she would think about it. That way you could visit any time you want."

"Sounds like a good idea. Think of what movie you want to see and which of your friends you want to bring. Then we'll set a time to go see a movie and have some pizza."

"And maybe go to the SPCA. I gotta go. I have a soccer game today. Bye."

"Thanks again, Katie," he yelled after her as she ran down the sidewalk back to her house.

Back inside he went to the kitchen, grabbed the phone and then dialed Gabby's home number. The answering machine clicked on with the familiar message, John hung up and then dialed her office number.

"Hello?" Gabby's voice came through strong and confident.

"Hi."

"John!"

"I was going to take the day off to rest and forget about things but my curiosity got the better of me. Apparently yours did the same to you."

"It did. I figured those guys in the parking lot were a pretty powerful bunch. I was right."

"What do you mean?"

"Brogan's gone. The word is he's gone for good. The rumor is that he had a nervous breakdown. A total schizophrenic break. Everybody's acting like they knew it was coming. You know all those outbursts and irrationality. Like those were anything new. But in any case, people are buying into the story."

"What about David?"

"Now that's an interesting story. David is on vacation. He took his whole family to guess where."

"The Caribbean?"

"Nope. China."

"Somebody's got a sense of humor. David hated to travel." John laughed.

"Yeah, definitely. You know, though, I think we'll be seeing the real David around soon. If the real David wasn't coming back I think there would have been a different story. Maybe he'll get a liver transplant or something."

"Oh, sure. The technology is there to fix him. What's the word on me?"

Gabby hesitated for a long time.

"The jury's still out on you, John. I wouldn't come back just yet. There are signs that the storm clouds are clearing, though. The Board of Medicine seems to be backing off and the other state agencies are, too. I think the attempts to tag you with a criminal act are dying away."

"That leaves the malpractice suit."

"Eva Bentley's crazy brother is going full steam ahead there. What happened to Brogan just seems to have fired him up even more. However, there is a tiny light on the horizon."

"What's that?"

"There is another rumor, and I don't know where it's coming from…"

"Our new friends?"

"An obvious choice but who knows? This rumor says that Eva died because of a ruptured artery in her brain that made her stop breathing."

"That's a little closer to the truth. Is anyone buying into it?"

"A few."

"Well, that's not going to get me out of the malpractice suit."

"No it won't, but it might help your reputation. Let me tell you. At this point it needs a lot of help."

"I can imagine. I'm sure people are saying I fled town to escape the scandal of my misdeeds."

"Of course. Some heads are turning a different way even if it's not toward the truth."

"Unfortunately, the truth is not going to come out."

"I know. We have our promise."

"Oh, well. It would be nice to think that we could have saved the world."

"I think we've done enough already. That man said so. We lead the authorities right to the bad guys."

John smiled briefly.

"You still, there, John?"

"Sorry. I got lost in thought."

"Well, nothing has changed here for me. I still have loads of work to do. Talk to you later. We'll have dinner soon."

"Or breakfast. Bye."

Later that day John talked to his lawyers. They heard his voice with relief and peppered him with questions. His answers, out of necessity, were not very forthcoming. They informed him that the case against him had about a fifty per cent chance of success but felt they could, with another month or two of hard work, whittle this chance down to about forty per cent but probably no better than that. If John were willing to pay a lot more money they could bring on an expensive, but very capable lawyer who would greatly increase the chances for success. The anger and frustration from the Bentley family was beginning to mount. The brother in particular appeared to want to take the case as far as possible against John. He was refusing to discuss a settlement. Furthermore, he was threatening all kinds of appeals if the case didn't fall his way. Thus John could be facing a long drawn-out series of court battles that could take years and lots of money. What did John want them to do?

He thought about the situation for a day and then called them back.

"Get the lawyer," he told them, "whatever the cost. I want someone to have me exonerated. Facts are facts. I had no part in her death. I feel sorry for the brother and the family but their vendetta is directed against the wrong person." Stunned his lawyers agreed. They needed an advance of $50,000 dollars for the next three months. The sum shook John. He didn't have it and thus would have to go the bank to borrow the money. He couldn't imagine what years of court battles would bring the amount to ultimately.

The following day a lawyer from the hospital called him at home.

"Dr. Bishop," he said. "I'm John Folger from the firm of Folger and Petersen. I represent the hospital in the suit brought by the Bentley family against you and the hospital. I have what I think is good news. The family has agreed to settle. The total amount I can't disclose, but the hospital is willing to accept this figure on the condition that you pay what, I think, you will consider to be a reasonable amount."

"What would that be?"

"$10,000."

Silence. Inwardly John felt elated but remained doubtful.

"And that would be the end of this whole situation?"

"The lawsuit would be over and done with. At least as far as this was concerned, yes. The family would be prohibited from bringing any further action against you or the hospital."

John was smiling now.

"Does this constitute an admission of guilt?"

"No. None whatsoever."

"I'll take this deal. I'll have to talk to my lawyers, but basically I agree to it."

"Excellent, Dr. Bishop. That is good news. We'll be waiting to hear from you. Good-bye."

The man hung up. John looked around his room. Invisible hands were taking his life and putting it back together. He didn't know what to think. He sank into his sofa and felt his body relax like it hadn't done in a long while. The promise of a normal life began to dawn within him. Was it possible? Was the nightmare over? He called Gabby at the hospital and told her the news.

"Well, doesn't that beat everything! We go through all that hell and then in the snap of a finger it's all fixed!"

"I'm not going to argue with it."

"Neither am I. It's just hard to let your guard down when it seems the whole world is out to ruin or kill you."

"I know what you mean. Still, it's time to celebrate. Dinner together at Chez Michel?"

"Absolutely! We'll have a bottle of good champagne."

"This Saturday at 8. I'll pick you up at your place."

"It's a deal."

They both hung up feeling elated. John began to think about going back to work. A phone call to the interim CEO brought encouraging results. The administrator sounded startled and puzzled at first. After a pause said he would look into the possibility of reinstating his hospital privileges since the events surrounding Eva Bentley's death appeared to have been misconstrued by a large number of people to John's disadvantage. John added more details, which the CEO hadn't heard, and got the distinct impression that the chief administrator actually wanted him to come back but was proceeding cautiously. The administrator promised to give him a final word in a week. Slowly his old life was coming back together. Just days before it had appeared irretrievably ruined.

Saturday night John and Gabby had dinner together united through a bond formed through their recent experiences. They laughed and joked over the events of the past weeks and toasted their success with champagne. Gabby frequently reached over to touch John's hands and when they walked out of the restaurant they had circled their arms around each other.

"Good-bye, John. It's nice to have a fun evening out after what we've been through."

"It's nice not to have to keep looking over your shoulder."

"Am I going to see you back at work next week?"

"I'm waiting to hear from your new boss. What's he like?"

"Young, for a CEO. He's a hotshot MBA from Northwestern. A little cocky, too, but nice to work with. And guess what?"

"What?"

"You've been approved to come back. The medical staff met on Friday with administration. It was really just a formality. Bye, John."

He bent down and kissed her for one brief, sweet moment. Her eyes turned towards his face and held his gaze for a moment. Then he watched her wistfully as she disappeared into her car and then drove away. His feelings caught in his throat as the thought came to him that perhaps he should never have let her go, never have formed any hard feelings of bitterness, never should have given up so easily. On the drive home the feeling of regret haunted him.

After parking his car in his driveway he got out, slammed the car door shut and, out of habit, looked around. Across the street a yellow porsche caught his attention. Perhaps his neighbor, a fanatic for sports cars, had lost his head and bought the expensive car. The quiet of his neighborhood filled him with pleasure now that danger didn't seem to lurk in every shadow. The maple tree stood silently. The bushes were dark and unmoving. The night air was crisp and refreshing. To himself he smiled. He lived slightly in the country and savored that hint of nature that the countryside brought to him. As he walked to the front, door a voice from the shadows, to the right of his garage, stopped him dead.

"Dr. Bishop."

Where had he heard that voice?

"Over here, Dr. Bishop. I suggest you listen."

Out of the shadows stepped a woman with long, dark hair, a woman who once again startled and, despite his inner misgivings, dazzled him with her beauty. Eva Bentley stood before him brandishing an automatic pistol.

John struggled to control his fear and spoke calmly. "Eva, I am surprised but not surprised to see you still alive. I should have guessed. You're too smart to die so easily."

"And too valuable. The organization was beginning to fear that they would lose me. My work has brought them incredible sums of money and, until you came along, brought the organization a lot more security. So what you are thinking is right."

"Your clone died in the hospital," John finished.

"She was supposed to die earlier. I was trying to activate the microchip in her brain earlier but she got smart and figured things out. I suppose she got a little too much of my intuition and intelligence. Normally clones are rather docile, but as you can see, I am not a docile person and enough of that transferred to her. I had to chase her down that Maryland road and almost got close enough, but she got in an accident and all those people came out. Imagine what they would have thought had I walked out of my car."

A smile flickered on her lips.

"We made sure she got into one of our hospitals."

"I was wondering about that."

"Yeah, well, Brogan then tipped me off and the rest was easy. I came onto the ward that night and activated the device. You were the perfect set up."

"I almost had you."

Eva smiled in answer. "In this business almost doesn't cut it. My family wasn't supposed to get involved. That was the deal I had with the organization, not that they care much about my feelings. But that arrangement was convenient for them, too. I had to come tonight because my brother is now on his way to kill you, vigilante style, for the death of his sister. I can't allow him to do that. Not that you aren't supposed to die. Only my brother can't be found responsible for that. The investigations have to stop. The organization wants all this notoriety to die down. Brogan has been an idiot, and if you hadn't gotten him, we would have. So, Dr. Bishop, this is it."

She raised her gun toward his chest. Then another voice came from behind them, a man's voice. They both turned around to see a man coming toward them, one they both recognized as her brother. He had a large handgun and, surprisingly, it was pointed at Eva.

"I originally came here to kill Dr. Bishop, but I can see that I have been grossly mistaken in my understanding of events. I owe you a great apology for all the trouble I've caused you, Dr. Bishop. Eva, as you know, I love you and the family loves you, but I have learned more about you in the last minute than I have in a lifetime.

I can't let you continue this life you have chosen. I want you to put down that gun and come with me."

"Tony, you ought to leave right now."

"I can't. All I can think about is what went wrong. You were the star in the family, blessed with talents the rest of us could only dream of. Now look at you."

In the blink of an eye Eva's foot shot out catching her brother in the chest causing him to raise his arm and let off a shot whose report resounded through the neighborhood. She also caused him to stumble back a few steps. As Eva was turning around trying to train her gun once again on John, the brother regained his balance and leapt on her back pulling her down toward the ground. They struggled for only an instant until John heard a muffled sound as the brother sank back, lifeless, blood pooling on the ground from a wound in his chest. A siren started to blare in the distance. Eva looked up with fear, and then like a frightened animal ran to the yellow porsche and drove off. The phone began to ring in his house.

It rang and rang and clearly the caller was not going to hang up unless the phone was answered. Reluctantly he went into the house and picked up the phone.

"Yes?"

"Dr. Bishop, do not go out of your house for the next hour. Do not go near or look out your windows." The man on the other end hung up.

For the next hour he paced nervously around his kitchen with his dogs following him wagging their tails expectantly. A glass of wine remained untouched on the counter. Finally an hour had passed and he went cautiously back outside to greet a night as calm as in the first moments he had come home. No trace remained of Eva's brother. The blood that had stained the concrete was gone. No strange cars stood in the road.

Chapter XIX

The next day his phone rang insistently.

"Hello?"

"John. Strange news." It was Gabby. "Eva Bentley's brother was in a car accident last night and burned up with his car. Quite a tragedy."

"Burned up? Oh," he said vaguely.

"That's it? Oh?"

"I'll explain later."

"You sound strange."

"Well, I feel strange."

"John, what the hell are you talking about?"

"How about breakfast tomorrow morning and I'll explain. Our usual place."

"Ok. Seven o'clock then. See ya."

John sat morosely at a booth at O'Toole's breakfast diner. He stared at his cup of black coffee as the steam rose up from it. In an unusual feat of punctuality at 7 o'clock sharp, Gabby came into the restaurant, bouncy and happy, and then plopped down beside John instead of her usual spot opposite him.

"C'mon, John. Cheer up. You don't have to be so serious anymore."

"Sorry. I'm feeling a little bit responsible for a man's death."

"Oh yeah? Whose."

"Bentley's brother."

Gabby frowned.

"It's not your fault he had a car accident. I think that's taking things a little too personally."

"He didn't die in a car accident. He died at my house last night. Eva was there first. She was the one who activated the microchip and killed her clone on the rehab unit. Brogan helped her."

"Eva? Amazing."

"She came to kill me and would have, but her brother got there, too, and she and her brother had a struggle and Eva's gun went off and killed him."

"I should have guessed the car accident was a coverup. It was too convenient. Why didn't Eva kill you?"

"No time. Once her brother's gun went off, the neighborhood woke up and she had to get out of there fast."

"So how was she compared to her clone?"

"I learned something rather strange. There is a huge difference between a clone and the original. A clone is pretty pale in comparison."

"I don't know, John. Your clone was, uh, pretty hot."

John considered this.

"Did you really like him?"

"Not that way. He wasn't you. The difference was obvious."

"You know, the real Eva, despite her waywardness, had a real presence about her. It's too bad she chose the wrong side."

"Doesn't seem to like you, does she?"

"Hates me. But that's not why I'm bummed out. I feel a bit responsible for her brother's death. He was innocent in all of this."

"So were you, John."

"Maybe."

"John, it's just the way it is. You know the saying, live by the sword, die by the sword."

John looked straight into Gabby's eyes. In those liquid pools of fire and emotion was real compassion. For a moment he was distracted.

"Perhaps you're right."

"Of course I'm right."

She put her arms around him and gave him a squeeze.

"John, listen. I've got something really interesting to tell you. I've been fooling around with the web. I plugged in Dragon's Tail and you'll never guess what I found."

"What else? Karate movies."

"Besides those. A fourteenth century prophetess born in England in a cave. Her name was Mother Shipton. She wrote prophecies in verse and became persecuted for them although many of them came true. Anyway she wrote about the dragon's tail as the evil that was supposed to bring down the world or could bring down the world."

"And you think that's our dragon's tail?"

"Who knows? Evil men with immense power playing with genetics for profit and gain and without any regard for the consequences… I'd say that was a bad recipe."

"Happening as we speak. Scary. I don't know about the Mother Shipton part, though."

John looked at her skeptically and then allowed himself to smile.

"Maybe it's just a strange coincidence," he said. "But here's a question for you. You saw a lot more in those labs than you've told me, right?"

"Yeah, and so did you."

"Of course. Well, what do think was the worst evil in terms of the clones that you saw down there."

"I saw a man who could be one of the most fearsome soldiers the world has seen. Physically incredible, programmed to obey, a brain with its frontal lobes or areas of moral concern reduced and with a high, mechanical type of intelligence."

"I saw him, too. He could be cloned to make a great army. That is true. But did you see that teenager, the slender, really attractive guy?"

"Yeah, so what? What was so special about him?"

"I think he had the greater evil."

"Why is that?"

"In their eagerness to make him, they accumulated cancer genes into his DNA and other defects. That boy was so attractive he and others like him probably would have reproduced and introduced genes that would have initiated a gradual deterioration of human gene structure."

"You mean generations from now humans would be grotesquely deformed?"

"Perhaps. I don't know. Maybe we would have evolved into a race with a defective immune structure. A very sickly race."

"Ok. The time for depression is over. We gave the bad guys a kick in the butt, and for now we're going to be happy. Ok?"

John laughed.

"Ok. But it's still out there."

"Yup. And perhaps there's not much more you and I can do about that. But if Eva Bentley hadn't come into your life, you and I would never have known and never would have had a chance to do at least something."

"It could have turned out just the opposite."

"That's the way life is. Fortunately things turned out well."

"The thing that's worries me is that for them to do so well in this genetics trade there must be a huge market in the legitimate and not so legitimate world of health."

"A lot of greedy people. They think the end justifies the means but it doesn't."

"Complete stupidity there. Once the genetic heritage of our species is lost, it will be lost perhaps to all future generations. All so a couple of fat cats like Brogan can get rich."

"Well, fortunately Brogan got busted."

"I did like talking to my clone."

"You're perverse."

"He seemed to like you."

"Perhaps clones are a little more romantic than their, uh, master copies."

There was an awkward silence.

"Maybe so," John whispered.

Gabby squeezed his hand.

"Just kidding, John."

For a moment the incredible bond that had held them together since Eva Bentley's death rose up within them and the unity they felt transcended all the animosities and fears and doubts that had previously pushed them apart. Uncharacteristically, Gabby looked down at the table almost as if she felt twinges of guilt.

"I don't know. Sometimes I feel like I wish we were still together."

Remorse gripped John, and he placed her hand between both of his.

"Blame me. I was the idiot in our relationship. I am not as stupid as I once was. Forgive me, Gabby. Give me a chance to start again."

"I don't think things work that way, not in the real world."

"We can test the waters. Nothing really serious unless things work out. Does that sound ok?"

Gabby looked away frowning.

"It's pretty hard to turn back the pages, John. You hurt my feelings pretty badly once. Trust can be hard to get back."

"We'll just try a little baby step and see what happens. C'mon. Let me take you out to dinner tomorrow. A real date. A fresh start. We're both different people after all we've been through."

Gabby looked at him doubtfully and then laid her head on his shoulder.

"One date. For old time's sake."

The smell of her hair made him dizzy. For a moment recent events faded into a cozy haze, and a part of him that had been pushed deep into some buried recess of his mind began to reemerge with new energy and a new sense of promise.

Chapter XX

"Damn!" John stared at the TV in dismay. Snow. Lots of it. A snowstorm was coming tonight. Perhaps Gabby would cancel. He didn't want to and couldn't wait to give her the surprise he had dreamed up for her and now here was snow about to put its crazy whiteness in his way. Usually it didn't come this early in the season. He gave her a quick call.

"Hi. There's a snowstorm coming."

"I know. You're not chickening out on me are you?"

"Perish the thought. How about you?"

"After what we've been through a little snow will be one of nature's welcome diversions. Is your car ok in the snow?"

"It's not great, but I'll be there. See you in an hour."

They said goodbye and hung up.

Except for one other couple and themselves the restaurant was empty. Soon after the appetizers the other couple left, and John and Gabby found themselves alone in one of the town's ritziest restaurants as a winter storm raged outside.

John addressed himself to the waiter.

"Sir, are we keeping everyone here from going home? Would it be better if we left so everybody here could go home?"

The waiter smiled and his eyes twinkled.

"Stay as long as you like. Everybody who is left here is going to spend the night at a hotel across the street. We'd be happy to serve you as long as you want. In fact the owner, in honor of you being our only guest on such a stormy night, would like to give you a complimentary bottle of champagne."

Gabby beamed.

"Thanks very much.

Moments later a bottle of Perrier-Jouet arrived in a champagne bucket, and after the waiter, after he pulled the cork with a happy pop, poured two bubbling glasses for each of them. John shyly pulled out a small, box wrapped in green and gold metallic paper.

"I guess this is as good a time as any to give you this. I wanted to express my appreciation for all the loyalty and help you've given me through all this. For a while there, you were my only friend and you risked a lot to help me. Thanks."

He reached over and placed the box in front of her as Gabby stared at the tiny present with wonder and curiosity.

"Sweet and thoughtful as always, John."

"Go ahead. Open it."

Gabby tore away the paper and lifted the lid off of the white box. She gasped with delight with what she saw inside. Nestled on a bed of cotton lay a pair of earrings sparkling with precious stones. She held them up to the light. Each earring was a gold dragon held upside down by its tail. In the mouth of each was mounted a single large diamond surrounded by emeralds. Platinum laced the dragons.

"They're beautiful, John. Just beautiful," Gabby said in a whisper. "But why are the dragons hanging upside down?"

"That's a symbol of their defeat and of our control over them. The diamonds represent purity and good over evil. Go ahead and put them on."

"Is that all they represent, good over evil?" Gabby said as she slipped the earrings on and began to admire them with a pocket mirror.

John thought for a moment.

"Of course not. They are also a symbol of my eternal affection and gratitude. Nobody in the world could ever match what you have done for me in these past weeks, some of the hardest in my life."

She looked at him and flashed him a dazzling smile.

"You do love me, John, don't you?" she asked quietly.

He stared into her eyes that flashed with energy and emotion.

"Of course I do."

Gabby raised a glass of champagne.

"I propose a toast then."

John raised his glass.

"I want to thank you for this gift. The past few weeks have been hard at times, but they have been some of the most fascinating and adventurous times of my life. I am glad I got to spend them with someone who can drive me crazy but who, also, is one of the sweetest men I know and whom I will always love very much."

They clinked glasses and drank.

"You're supposed to kiss me now," she teased.

Without the slightest trace of embarrassment he leaned over and kissed her for a long time. When they sat up they saw the waiters watching them, grinning.

An hour later they left the restaurant arm in arm and stepped into the winter storm as snowflakes floated down around them. The streets and sidewalks were empty of people. Their feet left deep prints in the snow, and the blanket of snow quieted all sound.

"Are we going to get home tonight?"

"Sure. My car can get through this. The trucks should be around soon. Here's the car. Why don't we get in, wait for the plows to clear the road. Then I'll dig it out and we'll leave."

John helped Gabby into the darkened car. The windows were completely covered in snow and blocked the light from the streetlamps. John slipped into the driver's seat.

"I can't start up the engine or else the exhaust might come back in."

"Well, then come get close to me and hold my hands. They're cold."

He put each hand between his and rubbed them until the warmth had come back a little and then playfully kissed her on the neck.

Her arms swung around him, and all rational thought melted in a turbulence of passion, of old feelings and new, of ambivalence and certainty as the snow fell around them on the city streets.

"John, not so rough."

"What's the matter?"

"You're shaking the car it's making me feel sick."

"I am not doing anything."

"Then what's going on?"

Sure enough the car was jostling roughly and they could feel the front of it rising and the sound of metal creaking.

John switched on the wipers. When they windows cleared they both burst into laughter.

"It's a tow truck. We're being towed."

Their laughter rang loudly in the car although nobody heard them. They sank back into their seats and into each other's arms.

The man walked quickly away from the town. The rain beat heavily upon the ground and soon turned the road into mud. However, the freshness of the rain and the attainment of his freedom filled him with immense joy. Although he had seen the king smile, he had also seen the cold glint of hatred and fear as the ambitious monarch pronounced his freedom. The king was not a merciful man and surely had no intention of granting him his freedom. Any moment now the soldiers might come upon him with the speed of their horses and thrust their spears through his heart or cut him down with their swords. Looking behind him he only saw the country road. Without a second thought he turned off the road and plunged deep into the forest to head for the hilly regions. There he lived for the rest of his life alone. Every now and again a villager would find his way to him to have a wound healed, a fracture set or some other malady healed. Very rarely the man would slip into the village at night to help a man or woman who might die, but as soon as he could, he went back into the forest where the trees were his friends, the sound of the streams his music and the wind the soft caress of love. And when he died, his story grew into a legend as the hermit who knew the ways of nature and could heal the sick.

Dedication

Dedicated to Max and Kali, lovebugs forever.

For Elain, l'amour principale.

Dedicated to Carlitos for your continuing and generous love and support.

Herein are the greatest hopes for progress in science and medicine towards cures for neurological injury.

Acknowledgements

Doug Murphy
I would like to express my gratitude to my wife, Elain Heffelfinger, for her help and support in the preparation of this manuscript.

My mother, Dimitria Murphy, has provided abundant encouragement and inspiration.

Andrea Murphy
I would like to thank my entire family for their love and friendship and a special thanks to my brother.

Printed in the United States
2873